ONE STORMY NIGHT

SOFIA SAWYER

CITY OWL
PRESS

ONE STORMY NIGHT
Her Journey, Book 1

CITY OWL PRESS
www.cityowlpress.com

Cover Design by Mibl Art. All stock photos licensed appropriately.

Edited by Mary Cain.

For information on subsidiary rights, please contact the publisher at info@cityowlpress.com.

Print Edition ISBN: 978-1-64898-081-7

Digital Edition ISBN: 978-1-64898-082-4

Printed in the United States of America

To the insatiably curious.
Keep learning. Keep exploring. Keep discovering.

ALSO BY SOFIA SAWYER

No Place to Hide

Always, Ella

Saving the Winchester Inn

CHAPTER ONE

"HE'S *SO* HOT."

"The things I'd do to him."

Hiding in the far corner of the break room, Charlie Middleton hunched over her snack as the two women from marketing shared their explicit fantasies shamelessly without a care in the world as to who overheard. Charlie cringed as their high-pitched giggles reverberated against the walls of the near-empty room.

Jada bit her bottom lip as she stared at the TV mounted on the wall. "He's starred in at least a dozen of my dreams. *Wet* ones."

Charlie tried to take a bite of her coveted yogurt, which had lost its allure thanks to the X-rated conversation a few tables over. After hearing bits and pieces of those "wet dreams," Charlie stared at thick white goop on her spoon, unable to stomach it.

He was Lachlan Hart, their CEO, the founder of MindThrive AI —an extremely successful artificial intelligence and machine learning tech company.

Charlie sighed and frowned, accidently catching the eye of one of the women. Ducking her head, she sank farther in her seat until she was nearly half under the table. Finding a brief break in her insane schedule was a luxury she rarely got, so she hoped the fleeting eye-lock didn't cause the women to include her in their chatter. All she wanted was ten measly minutes to herself without anyone needing something from her. Just ten blissful moments of silence.

No such luck.

"Oh, Charlie!" Noelle called out.

Charlie reluctantly sat up and gave a tight smile, now wishing she had stayed at her desk like usual. Why she thought a field trip to the community break room would be a good idea was beyond her.

It will be healthy to get away from your desk, she had argued with herself. *A change of scenery is just what you need.*

She snorted at the thought. *Yeah, right.*

As much as she loved the airy, sleek spaces of the office's industrial-modern open floor plan, it was impossible to take an uninterrupted breather. Maybe Noelle would make it quick, and she could go back to her snack in peace.

Her stomach turned. *Maybe not.*

"What's it like to work for Lachlan?" Noelle pressed without waiting for Charlie to acknowledge her.

Noelle twirled a section of silky blond hair around her finger, the look on her face one of wistful lust. It was a look Charlie had become accustomed to seeing whenever her boss was brought up in conversation.

Or was in a woman's presence.

Or some men's, for that matter.

Lachlan Hart was a man of many people's dreams. If only they knew him like she did. They'd steer clear.

Jada chimed in. "What Noelle means is how do you not give in to the urge to rip his clothes off?" Raising a perfectly sculpted eyebrow, she added, "Or have you already?"

Both women leaned forward expectantly, waiting for the juicy gossip.

Charlie tried not to roll her eyes while she straightened and raised her chin higher. Placing her yogurt on the table, she cleared her throat in preparation to give her practiced speech, one she perfected throughout the last three years she'd worked for Lachlan. She sucked in a deep breath, ready to rattle it off as quickly as she could.

"He's a generous man," she started in a poised, professional voice.

When he wasn't working so relentlessly and took a second to see what was around him.

"So ambitious. Clearly dedicated to his work. I've learned a lot from him."

Whether I wanted to learn or not. Through the long hours, constant demands, and high expectations, she had to step it up. For many, working for "tech genius" Lachlan Hart was a once-in-a-lifetime opportunity. For her, it was soul-sucking, exhausting work that left her with no energy to focus on her own life.

"And although I have to agree he *is* very easy on the eyes"—the comment made the women giggle again—"he's been nothing but a professional. A wonderful boss."

Well, the good-looking and ambitious parts were true. Everything else was a bit of a stretch. Lachlan had worked her hard over the years, and although it was tough, it at least opened doors for her.

Doors she intended on taking.

It was time she got her life back. After years of catering to Lachlan, putting him before herself, she was taking a stand.

Noelle looked like she had sucked on a lemon, and Jada was scrolling on her phone, no longer listening. The women were clearly disappointed by her prudish response. Bored with her, they went back to their own discussion, ignoring Charlie again.

She breathed out a sigh of relief, glad she'd shut that down so quickly. It might have been a record. But before she had a chance to pick up her unappetizing lunch again, her phone dinged with a text.

Lachlan Hart: *Reschedule our noon meeting. Have driver take me to the new address. Check email.*

Charlie snapped her head toward the flat-screen TV. Lachlan was in deep discussion with a CNN interviewer, explaining how MindThrive's artificial intelligence worked.

"This is live, isn't it?" she asked.

"Yup. But I'm recording it at home. You know, just in case I need some inspiration on those lonely nights." Noelle winked unabashedly.

Charlie's eyebrows furrowed. She turned back to the screen, finding Lachlan's piercing cerulean eyes staring at her with the same intensity that always made her feel like she didn't measure up. She tried not to squirm under their scrutiny and failed.

How does he do that? And didn't they tell him to never look directly at the camera?

She made a call to his driver and texted him a confirmation.

Lachlan Hart: *Thank you.*

She looked to the TV again where he was giving a demo of their new product features coming out next month. No phone in sight.

Seriously, how does he do that?

"Hey, girl." Devonny Mercado, Charlie's friend from college, current roommate, and MindThrive's human resources manager, strolled into the break room.

Noelle and Jada's chatter stopped abruptly as they eyed Devonny. Without hesitation, they stood and scurried out of the room, their designer heels clicking on the polished concrete floor.

Devonny made a face, tossed her thick black hair over her shoulder, and took a seat at the table. "Let me guess. They were objectifying our fearless leader again." She pursed her lips and rolled her eyes with the kind of attitude only she could pull off.

Charlie smiled at her friend's ability to cut through the bullshit. It was one of the reasons Charlie was so drawn to her during their first year at NYU. Devonny was her own woman: intelligent, independent, inspiring, and fierce. She was a strong woman in Charlie's corner, which proved helpful when she moved to New York for college after growing up in quaint Savannah, Georgia.

Culture shock was an understatement, but Devonny always had her back.

"Would you expect anything else?"

"It's insane how women fall at his feet." Devonny shook her head, her thick waves bouncing with the movement. "If more women took time to focus on themselves and their careers rather than daydream about someone *so* unattainable, maybe the world would be a better place."

Devonny was a feminist, dreaming of a world run by powerful women. Of course, that dream deflated whenever she witnessed things like that.

"You mean Mr. Personality? What's not to like?" Charlie deadpanned, causing them both to laugh, knowing full well the ins and outs of working closely with Lachlan.

Charlie often wondered if being a bit eccentric was a requirement for becoming a rich tech genius. Lachlan was definitely *particular.* There'd been many times when she was tempted to muss his perfect dark hair—always pushed back and parted on the side in that stylish way featured in men's upscale fashion magazines—loosen up his tie, and tell him to get over himself.

It wasn't that Lachlan was self-absorbed or cruel, per se, but he did everything with precision. His communication style, both in-person and digitally, was short and concise. And although he often rubbed elbows with people in the tech community, he kept a cool distance, never giving away too much of himself. Somehow, he'd managed to stay out of the spotlight unless it specifically dealt with the company he built with his partner, Matteo Maggio. He rarely got personal. Matteo truly was the only one who knew him.

To everyone else, he remained a mystery. Even the women who occasionally escorted him to events were kept at arm's length. His aloofness—and to be honest, his bank account—made him a sought-after bachelor. They wanted to be the special one who was brought into the fold. Yet he stayed unattached. A lone wolf.

Charlie had worked for him for three *long* years, filled with early mornings, late nights, and plenty of weekends. She'd assumed spending that much time with someone would allow her to learn something about that person.

Not when it came to Lachlan Hart.

If she could describe him best, he was a robot. A beautiful, brilliant robot. Expressionless and efficient.

In fact, Charlie wasn't sure she'd ever seen him smile. Sure, he'd share a polite grin here or there. But a full-blown, reach-his-eyes smile was not something that fit in Lachlan's world. He was a serious man, hyperfocused on his work, and he had the success to show for it.

"I bet you're excited to give your official resignation." Devonny's Cheshire cat grin reminded Charlie of the big step she was about to take.

She crinkled her nose. "He canceled on me. Asked me to push our meeting."

"What? Oh no, girl. You better get back on that schedule pronto. You know how he is."

"You're right. And as ruler of his calendar..." Charlie pulled up his schedule on her phone and scrolled through. "I'll make a few adjustments to his afternoon. He can't avoid this conversation no matter how hard he tries." She made a couple of clicks and confirmed it.

"Good. The more time he has to sit with this, the better. I've spent the past two weeks scouting potential replacements, although you know no one will come close to you." She winked.

Charlie blushed. "I'm not that great."

"Are you kidding? You're the first assistant who's lasted this long. He's either scared them off or asked them to be removed because they practically sexually assaulted him." She gave a dry laugh. "I think the record before you was nearly a year. Lachlan is as precise as he is demanding. You cracked his code somehow—pun not intended—and found a way to give him what he needs, all without losing your damn mind in the process."

Charlie pointed to her head. "Do you see these grays? That's from him."

Devonny chuckled and stood to leave. "Even if you did have grays, it's not going to show up in that gorgeous red hair of yours. Anyway, keep me posted."

Charlie's phone buzzed again, alerting her that the CNN interview was over and Lachlan was now on his crazy spree of requests. She scrolled through several messages and sighed. What he needed from her would lead well into the night.

"Guess I have to cancel the first date I've had in a while." She sank in her chair and frowned.

Devonny squeezed her shoulder. "In a month, when you're kicking ass at the UX bootcamp, things will be different. You'll have your life back and all the time in the world to go on dates. Or do anything, for that matter."

"I hope you're right. Because quitting Lachlan Hart may be my hardest challenge yet."

* * *

Charlie took a cleansing breath as Lachlan stepped out of the sleek black town car onto the bustling sidewalk in SoHo. People parted like the Red Sea as he walked purposefully to the front doors of a beautiful sixteen-story structure from the 1920s that still possessed the charm from that time but was now home to MindThrive's high-tech renovations of the future.

She had heard him once tell an investor how he liked the symbolism of the building: pushing forward while still "remembering where you came from. Melding old with new." Lachlan rarely revealed much about himself as he had in that brief conversation. It had almost made him seem a little more normal. Relatable. Accessible. She had held on to that memory during their more *trying* times.

People were quick to step aside and let him by, allowing him to push through the revolving door. He was a force of nature. Yet no matter how smart he was, he was oblivious to the orbit around him.

Lachlan's footsteps echoed off the lobby's polished floors, and he brushed by Charlie—waiting for him as always—at the elevator bank. Charlie hadn't expected a warm greeting. If Lachlan was one thing, it was focused, sometimes to the point where he could completely shut out the world around him. She learned not to take offense when he barely acknowledged her.

Kind of.

She had worked hard over the years to be efficient, meeting his high expectations in a way he'd found invaluable. Or so he'd told her once in passing. Out of all the assistants he'd had, Charlie had found a way to blend into his life seamlessly, anticipating his needs before he had to ask, which was probably how she had survived in the role for as long as she had.

Barely.

Perfectly reliable. Always there.

He punched the button to the sixteenth floor and then jammed the close button. Charlie hopped in just before the doors could smush her in the process. She straightened her pencil skirt, trying not to show her annoyance, and used the short ride to get him up to speed on what he missed while he was out.

A knot formed in her stomach as she thought about her resignation. Only a few more minutes—when they were in the privacy of his office—and she'd finally tell him she was moving on. How he'd react was anyone's guess, if he reacted at all.

She swallowed a lump in her throat and pushed back a strand of her hair that had fallen loose from her usual tight bun. "The VC firm's legal department sent over paper work for review."

"Have Sue from legal look it over." He stared straight ahead at the closed doors.

"Already sent to her." She checked something off one of her many to-do lists she lived and died by. "The *New York Times* reached out about doing a spotlight piece on you."

He cringed.

"I asked them to send the questions over. I'll have PR respond and send headshot options," she said without missing a beat.

"Good," he said, his voice a steady monotone.

"Someone from Monmouth Beach Elementary School called to see if you'd come in and speak to the students about careers in

STEM." She looked up with furrowed eyebrows. "Monmouth Beach sounds familiar. Isn't that your hometown?"

He paused and shot a quick glance at her. "It is."

Charlie shook her head and looked at her to-do list again. "I told the woman your schedule won't allow it. And it won't. I updated your calendar this afternoon and blocked off time to prep for the US Air Force deal in a couple weeks. You also have a meeting with the heads of R&D tomorrow morning. They're concerned about the timing for the new feature rollout."

The elevator dinged and opened to the top floor. They stepped off and took a shortcut through the winding pathways between desks, conference rooms, and collaboration spaces. Some people ducked their heads as they saw them coming, pretending to be model employees. A few women poked their heads out of their cubicles and sneaked a glance as Lachlan walked by. He ignored them and headed straight to his office.

Charlie followed, trying to keep up with his long strides. She'd been busy today, and although it was nearly five, there still was a ton to do.

Thanks to him.

But none of that would matter if she could just tell him she was done.

Finished. Over. Gone.

They reached her desk that sat outside his office, a large space with walls made entirely of glass. She picked up a cup of black coffee and handed it to him. A year ago, she'd mastered timing it so it was hot without being scalding. He'd never said he appreciated it, but the faint smile on his lips as he took that first sip told her he did.

Maybe.

He murmured a thanks and entered his office. She slipped the resignation letter off her desk as she followed, letting him settle in before she bombarded him with the news. Taking a seat, Lachlan scanned the color-coded paper work laid out on his desk. It was Charlie's system, organized in the order of importance.

"I finished most of the things you needed to be done from me today. I still have a couple hours left. Anything you want me to prioritize over another?"

He took a sip of his coffee and pinched the bridge of his nose, his tell when he had a tension headache coming on, which didn't bode well for her. She sucked in a breath, the paper shaking slightly in her hands.

"Doesn't matter. Just get it all done today."

Charlie pressed her lips together, and her cheeks flushed. "Mr. Hart." Her voice shook. She cleared her throat, trying to gather the confidence she needed to face him. "There's something I want to discuss with you."

He exhaled and rubbed his forehead, not bothering to meet her eyes. "Can it wait, Charlie?"

"Actually, it can't—" she responded, now distracted by her ringing desk phone. "Hold on a sec." She made it to her desk in two strides and snatched up the phone. "Mr. Hart's office."

"Charlie." Her mother's voice was filled with heartbreak, making the hair on Charlie's neck stand up.

She peered over her shoulder to see if Lachlan was listening. "Is everything okay? What's going on?" she asked in a frantic whisper.

"It's Aunt Violet. She's...she passed away this morning."

The resignation letter slipped from Charlie's fingers. She shook her head, tears filling her eyes. "What?" The question came out as a harsh croak. "How?"

"A blood clot. We never saw it coming. Vi said she felt under the weather last night. I offered to take her to the doctor after work today if she still felt poorly. It was too late. We should have gone last night." Her mother let out a painful sob.

Charlie's heart shattered in her chest, and her head felt dizzy. The room got smaller. Everything was in tunnel vision.

Raised in a highly religious community in the Georgia Bible Belt, her aunt had been like a second mother to her when Charlie's mother,

Gloria, was disowned by her parents for getting pregnant in high school.

Aunt Violet was a huge part of Charlie's life. The news of her passing destroyed her. She tried to suck in air, but her chest constricted.

This can't be real.

The shock of it made her feel like she was watching someone else's life.

And God, how she wished it were someone else's life.

Not Aunt Violet. Why?

"Please come home." Her mother's plead was a quiet whisper.

"I'll be there soon, Mama."

Charlie hung up her phone with a shaky hand. Her insides ached. She wanted to stay frozen and run away at the same time, anything to avoid the emotional turmoil threatening to take over. Her fight-or-flight instincts kicked in. In a rush to leave, she gathered what she could from her desk and ran-walked down the hall, skidding around the corner to Devonny's office to let her know it was her last official day. Devonny was nowhere to be found.

I'll just tell her when she gets home later. She'll understand.

As of now, she only had one thing on her mind: getting back to Savannah.

CHAPTER TWO

THE NEXT TWO days were a roller coaster of emotions, a mixture of intense sadness and empty numbness. Charlie stood by her mother's side as they watched the casket descend into the ground. She felt hollow, like a shell of who she once was. Each inch the casket disappeared, the more the crushing sensation of loss swallowed her.

The funeral was hard on both of them. Even with the cheery, bright Georgia sun beating down, Charlie's world had gone dark. Aunt Violet had always been there to offer encouragement and a laugh, often lightening the mood whenever Charlie had been hurt, upset, or heartbroken. She could use her aunt's positive energy now as she struggled to say good-bye.

Wrapping her mom in her arms, silent tears flowed down their cheeks. Her mother's body shook like a fallen leaf in the autumn wind. Fragile. Lost. On more than one occasion, Charlie had to catch Gloria when her knees buckled. Charlie had seen her mother cry before, but nothing like this.

This was unbearable.

After they thanked those who attended the funeral, Charlie drove them into town and parked near the visitor center, just a short walk to Aunt Violet's lawyer.

Gloria pulled down the visor and flipped open the mirror compartment. She dabbed at her eyes, fixing her smudged mascara. "It doesn't feel the same. I keep expecting her to come breezing through the door after her shift at the hospital."

Although Charlie had moved to New York nearly a decade earlier, and her uncle Jon had passed away four years ago, her mother and aunt remained together in the house Charlie had grown up in. Their bond had only become stronger through the years.

Charlie shifted in the driver's seat to glance at her mother. With the same dark-red hair and green eyes, it was like staring into a mirror. Her mom had always said she got her looks and spirit from the Middleton side, but her savvy and passion from her father.

Though, looking at her mother now, Charlie saw how the years had taken their toll. That lively spirit waned.

Had her laugh lines always been that deep? When did the grays overtake her beautiful, vibrant hair? What caused her eyes to lose a bit of their playful twinkle?

"Mama," Charlie said, her Southern accent more pronounced after being back in Georgia. "It's just us now." The words hung heavily between them.

Gloria squeezed Charlie's hand, fresh tears glistening in her eyes. "I know, baby."

"I don't feel right with you here all by yourself. I should come home."

Her mother gave her a stern look, the sadness disappearing for a moment. "Don't you dare. You worked hard to get where you are today, and you've finally found something you're passionate about. You're going to that camp thing."

"Bootcamp," Charlie corrected her with a smile.

"You're going to that bootcamp, and you're going to find yourself a wonderful career doin' that user whatever." A determined look was still planted firmly on Gloria's face.

"User experience."

Gloria waved a dismissive hand. "You know this technology stuff is beyond me. Even if I don't know what you're doin' or what it's called, I'm proud of you, baby. You're not givin' that up on account of me or anyone else. You grew up to be such a big-hearted, kind woman. Sometimes to a fault." She wagged a finger. "I've seen how you put others before yourself, but you need to know it's okay to be a little selfish for the things that matter to you. You've worked hard for this. Don't let it get pushed aside."

Charlie grimaced and bit her bottom lip. "Are you sure?"

"Have you taken a look in the refrigerator? I can't fit another casserole in there! Even the freezer is stuffed. Violet may be gone, but I still have my own family here. A community of wonderful friends. They'll be there for me." Gloria patted Charlie's leg.

Some of the guilt eased away, but the worry remained. "You'll call me whenever you need me though, right? With the new job, I'm bound to have more time. I'll visit as often as I can."

Gloria put a hand to Charlie's cheek and gave an appreciative smile. "How'd I get so lucky to have such a sweet girl?"

"I was raised by the best."

Gloria held her head high. "You sure were. Strong Southern women."

But as they got out of the car, the air of pride disappeared as soon as it came. Gloria's shoulders slumped, and the fire in her eyes dulled.

Charlie eyed her mom as she stuffed a few coins in the nearby parking meter. "Are you sure you don't want to do this another day?" She worried what the stress and grief would do to her mother. Gloria already looked so fragile. Charlie feared the visit with the lawyer would push her to the brink of deep depression.

Her mother intertwined their arms and gripped tightly as they made the short walk down Louisville Road to the lawyer's office, a historic Georgian-style house, constructed with antique brick and styled with a teal door and a gas lantern.

Gloria hesitated outside the door and sighed. "I need time to grieve and process. I'd rather get these things sorted so I have the freedom to do that."

Charlie's gut reaction told her not to trust her mother's strength, but rather than pressing further, she held back. Charlie didn't want to cause any more unnecessary stress, so she chose to respect Gloria's wishes. For now, at least. "If you're sure."

The women entered the building and found themselves in a tastefully decorated office. Charlie marveled over the craftsmanship of the wood around the doors and modeling. The chandelier and pendant medallion made the space feel luxurious without being pretentious. The foyer had been converted into a lobby where a young woman greeted him.

The receptionist rose, and Charlie couldn't help but admire her polished yet bold style. The woman's magenta blouse and gold jewelry looked gorgeous with her skin tone. Her dark hair fell in bouncy waves, framing her face and accenting her high cheekbones. With her height and graceful movements, she could have belonged on the runway for New York Fashion Week.

Charlie struggled to muster up a warm smile. "Hello. We're the Middletons, here to see Drake McRae."

"Yes, ma'am. He's expecting you." The woman's voice was soft and smooth, and held a Southern accent that reminded Charlie of years gone by. "Can I get you ladies anything? Water? Coffee?"

"Coffee would be great. Black for me. Cream and sugar for my mother."

"Decaf for me, please." Gloria, the grandmaster of civility, smiled and smoothed down the front of her black tweed jacket.

"Absolutely. Let's get you settled in Mr. McRae's office. I'll be by in just a bit with your coffee."

Charlie and Gloria followed the receptionist down the hall to a sizable room and took a seat in plush, cream-colored chairs. The late-afternoon sun streamed into the office, making it more welcoming despite their reason for being there. Windows looked out to the blooming crepe myrtles, adding pops of pink, white, and purple along the street. Spanish moss hung from the branches, swinging in the light breeze. The trees captured the attention of the occasional tourist stopping to snap a few photos before moving on.

A distinguished man in his sixties strolled into the room and offered them a handshake. With his seersucker suit, handkerchief, and a permanent sunglasses tan line, Drake McRae was a Southerner through-and-through. Charlie could easily picture him spending weekends on his boat with his grandchildren, enjoying the warm weather before the stifling heat of summer came.

"Ladies, thank you so much for comin'. My deepest condolences to you both." His voice held an accent only fit for the affluent.

The receptionist delivered their coffee, and Charlie welcomed the fresh scent of earthy aroma. All through college, she and Devonny would frequent a hole-in-the-wall coffee shop near their dorms. It was their go-to spot for everything: homework, socializing, bitchfests about boys, celebrations—you name it. The coffee was mediocre at best, but somehow the roasted beans produced the most addicting smell. Whenever she stepped into the shop and was hit with that scent, she was comforted.

Although the coffee she held now was nothing like bitter cups she and Devonny would down like water, the aroma comforted her all the same.

"Let's get down to business, shall we?" Mr. McRae said after a few minutes of pleasantries. He shuffled the files on his desk and pulled out a pair of reading glasses, holding the paper out while his eyes adjusted. "Mrs. Violet Radcliffe had written this will a little more than a decade ago while Jon was still with us." He flipped through some pages. "We do have amendments here, dated nearly a year ago."

As Drake read through some of the dry legal language, Charlie fought the urge to fall asleep. It had been a trying few days with a lot of running around, sleeplessness, and grief. She could have used this monotonous content on those restless nights. It would have knocked her out immediately.

"All right, now that the legal mumbo jumbo is out of the way, here's the part y'all are waitin' for," he finally said.

Charlie perked up, happy to know they'd be done here soon.

"Miss Gloria Middleton." He peered at her over the top of his glasses.

"Yes?" She wrung her hands and leaned forward. Charlie reached over and squeezed her mother's hand to settle her nerves.

"Violet has left you the house in Savannah, all her possessions—aside from a few pieces of family jewelry she's left for Charlie—and seventy percent of her life insurance policy payout."

Tears filled her eyes. "That's so generous of her. Although I don't know why I would expect anything different."

Mr. McRae took off his glasses for a moment and looked squarely at her and Charlie. "I've known Violet for many years. She loved you two so much. I'd reckon she'd've given you the world if she could've."

The tears spilled over. Her mother swallowed a hiccup. "Thank you. That's so kind of you to say."

"Of course." He smiled and put his glasses back on, flipping to the next page. "Miss Charlie Middleton." He cleared his throat and continued to read. "You'll receive thirty percent of the remainin' life insurance policy and the family jewelry in this safe-deposit box." He pushed a small, metal box across the desk without looking up and turned another page. "And lastly, Violet has left the Scottish cottage to you."

"Scottish cottage?" Charlie asked more to herself, trying to jog her memory. "The one she and Uncle Jon bought years ago?"

Drake flipped through some paper work, finding the deed and more information, and handed it to Charlie. "Looks like they purchased it seven years ago with the intention of fixin' it up for their retirement in the upcomin' years."

He slid her a photo of a two-story stone cottage with a matching stone-and-iron fence.

Recognition registered. "I vaguely remember this place."

Her mother leaned forward to peer at the picture. "She has a photo of it in her bedroom."

"That's right. I remember seeing it during one of my visits a few years ago. Where is this?" Charlie asked Drake.

"A small island called the Isle of Murdina." He shook his head as he struggled over the pronunciation. "It's a bit south of the Isle of Skye. Says here the house is located on Queen Mary Alley in a small village named Port Ophelia."

Charlie reviewed the information, her forehead scrunched in deep concentration. "You said they were fixing it up for their retirement?"

"From my understandin', it has some issues. Typical for a home as old as this." He sorted through more paper work and produced a business card. "Here. This is the information for the property manager, Kennedy MacFigeinn. He can tell you how much work has been done and what's left."

Charlie sank into her chair and looked at the picture of the charming cottage again. "Seems like that's going to be expensive and a lot of work. I don't know if I'll have the funds or the time to do that with my bootcamp coming up."

"The mortgage is already paid off, so it's up to you if you want to sit on it until you have free time to think it through. Violet also gave her blessin' if you'd rather sell. She knew it was a large commitment."

Charlie's heart clenched. Aunt Violet had told her about the cottage the day she and Uncle Jon had returned from their trip, saying the town and the beautiful home felt special to them. Magical.

Selling the cottage would mean she was selling a dream her aunt and uncle never got to see through. It would be like choosing to let go of a piece of them, the small bit that was left.

But realistically, she didn't have the financial resources to repair it. Sure, she had the money from the life insurance policy, but was it wise to sink it all into a house she might visit occasionally? That was, if the funds were even enough to cover the amount of work needed.

"Thank you. I'll give him a call," she said as she stuffed the card into her purse.

As they left the lawyer's office half an hour later, Charlie couldn't help the thoughts floating through her head. What was it about this unknown island that made her aunt and uncle fall so in love that they'd wanted to retire so far from home?

As the questions plagued her the rest of the evening, Charlie decided she'd have to go there and find out for herself.

CHAPTER THREE

"You don't have to rush this," Gloria suggested, her gaze darting back and forth as Charlie moved around the room. "I love havin' you here," she added while Charlie stuffed another item into her already overfilled suitcase. "Maybe you can stay a little while longer. The cottage isn't going anywhere."

Charlie jumped onto her suitcase, using her body weight to smush it enough so she could zip it closed. "I have to go now, Mama. Bootcamp starts in a couple of weeks, and I won't have time until the spring. And by then, I hope to have secured a job, so taking time off probably won't happen."

Gloria worried her bottom lip. "I just don't like you goin' all the way out there by yourself. What if somethin' happens to you?"

Charlie stopped fussing with her bag and faced her mother, hoping her smile would reassure her. "I'll be okay. They speak English there. Plus, I've taken self-defense courses. Can never be too careful as a woman in the city."

Gloria tried to smile, but the uncertainty lingered in her eyes. "You'll have enough time to come back before you have to return to New York?" she asked, her voice small.

Realizing her mother's nerves might also be fueled by spending her first night alone in the house since Aunt Violet had passed away, Charlie crossed the threshold of her childhood bedroom and gave her mom a tight hug. "I'll be there for a few days to meet with the property manager and see what I'm working with. One week max, and then I'll be on a plane back to Georgia to spend more time with you. Promise."

Gloria let out a sigh of relief, but her body was still tense. "Okay, baby."

Satisfied for now, Charlie went back to her suitcases. She stuffed new linens and a comforter into the empty bag sitting next to her carry-on. According to the property manager, the house had practically nothing in it. Aside from two stripped beds and a small bistro table for two, the place was empty but habitable, for the most part.

At least, that's what she thought he had said. His thick Scottish accent had been hard to understand at times.

Charlie was never one to rough it, but he at least confirmed the water and electricity were in working order when it didn't occasionally act up. That was enough for her.

"When do you land?"

"Around eight in the morning tomorrow. I have stopovers in Boston and Dublin." She cringed at the thought. A four-hour drive to Atlanta's airport and nearly fifteen hours of airports and planes were going to be exhausting after these past few stressful days, but they were the cheapest flights she could find on such short notice.

"And then what?" Gloria pulled out the linens and refolded them so they'd fit better in the bag.

"I'll take a bus to the Kennacraig port where I'll meet Kennedy, the property manager. We'll take the CalMac ferry to the island." She rattled off her game plan as she finished packing the last things in her suitcase.

"I see."

"Please don't worry," Charlie begged again. "Kennedy assured me that cell service works just fine out there. I'll text and call as often as I can. Okay?"

Gloria nodded. "You better get goin'. You don't wanna miss your flight. You know how traffic can be around Atlanta."

Charlie hoisted the backpack onto her shoulders and grabbed her carry-on and suitcase, placing a quick kiss on her mother's cheek as she slipped by. "I'll call you when I get to Edinburgh."

* * *

Nearly a day later, Charlie stood outside her hotel in Edinburgh. She was tired, but the city had breathed new life into her. She stared up at the eighteenth-century, Georgian-style building. The dark stone and ironwork made it easy to picture life in Scotland centuries ago.

She was due to meet Kennedy at the port tomorrow and wanted to take advantage of her first trip to Scotland. Her first trip in a while, actually. With her hotel in a prime location, Charlie was excited by the prospect of taking short walks to all the attractions New Town and Old Town had to offer.

Making her way up the stone steps, she rolled her bags into the elegantly decorated lobby, full of wood, stone, and pops of bright turquoise.

"Hello, Miss. Welcome to Hotel Indigo. How may I help ye?" The gentleman at the front desk spoke with a smooth Scottish accent.

"Hi. My name is Charlie Middleton. I'm checking in," she said as she struggled with her roller bag.

The man searched his computer and smiled. "For one evening, aye?"

"Yes."

"Grand. The room is nae ready until noon. Would ye prefer to have us hold your bags so ye are free to explore? Word of Mouth is a grand place for breakfast if ye are peckish."

"That would be perfect." Charlie handed off her unruly bags. "Am I able to get tickets for the Hop-on, Hop-off bus?"

"Absolutely. Perfect day for it. Nae a drop of rain in the forecast."

The gentleman led her to the concierge, who placed a few calls for her. Before she knew it, she was riding on top of a double-decker bus through the city, exploring the highlights of Edinburgh.

Although she had spent the summer between high school and college traveling overseas and did a semester abroad in Rome, she never found her way to Scotland. It had been on her bucket list, but once she got into the core of her career, trips like this were harder to make time for.

It was a shame, really. For Charlie, traveling had a way of opening her eyes and giving her a sense of clarity. After years of getting sucked into the "rat race," clarity was exactly what she needed. These last few years made her brain foggy, and as the days flashed by faster and faster, she worried she was missing something crucial in her life.

Lost in her thoughts, Charlie strolled along the Edinburgh Castle courtyards and stopped at the stone wall to view the city spanning below. The fall sun made the Firth of Forth sparkle as if it were filled with brilliant sapphires. She inhaled deeply, taking in the crisp air.

For the first time in a week, she was finally ready to process everything that had happened, and what a beautiful place to do it.

Aside from a few messages from Devonny checking in on her, she hadn't heard a peep from work. It made sense since she had given back her work cell, but had she not been so caught up with the grief of losing her aunt, the silence would have been unnerving.

She wondered how Lachlan had taken the news of her resignation and hoped she didn't burn any bridges by racing out without giving notice as she had planned. Devonny had promised to smooth things over. She was a good friend like that.

A bagpiper nearby lifted his instrument and expertly played a hauntingly epic song. Charlie was transported to the rich history of this country, the music evoking the sense of loyalty, honor, and adventure. In a way, the song was perfect for her at this moment. She was embarking on a great adventure herself, not just to Scotland to see her aunt's cottage, but in her life too. When she considered

Scotland, she thought of its people, full of strength and determination, something she aspired to be.

She had spent the beginning of her adult years living in uncertainty, unsure of which path was right for her, worrying she'd never find something that spoke to her.

Just as Charlie was about to make those decisions, Lachlan had selected her as his assistant, leaving her without a moment to even consider a future for herself. Maybe she was a late bloomer, but once she discovered what she wanted, she wasted no time putting the plan in motion. It took a while to save the money needed to attend the bootcamp, but she was committed to making it happen. Nothing was going to derail her from finally finding her place in life.

As Charlie gazed at the views in the far distance, her stomach fluttered. The beginning of a new chapter in her life's story was only mere weeks away. The abrupt change was disorienting, but she hoped this transition period from her old life would give her the confidence she needed to embrace her new one. She wanted to find purpose, something she had always longed for.

Something she believed was always meant for everyone else but her. That was about to change. She just knew it.

Charlie slipped a hand into her cross-body purse, pulling out a letter Drake had given to her at his office—a letter from Aunt Violet, dated nearly a year ago. Despite reading it four times, this moment was the right one to let her truly absorb what her aunt had tried to say. It was as if being in Scotland put her in the right frame of mind to accept that this letter was her aunt's last parting wisdom.

She unfolded the paper, focusing on the graceful penmanship. Aunt Violet really had the most beautiful handwriting.

Charlie,

If you're reading this, it means I went to be with your uncle Jon. I hope I would have had the opportunity to share all of this in person, but if not, I pray this letter will help you understand.

To say I love you doesn't come close to how I really feel. Despite the circumstances, I couldn't have been happier for how you and your mother came into our lives. It's been a joy watching you grow up into the smart, talented, and independent woman you are. I'd like to think that maybe I helped you along in that direction. After all, I see so much of myself in you, which is why you need to really listen to what I have to say.

I've lived a full life. Even though our little family has seen its hard times, I had everything I could ever want: a home filled with love, a husband who I fell more in love with each year we were together, and a daughter found in you. But as you know, life has a funny way of getting away from us.

Even now as I write this, I think of the things I wish I would have done: visited you in New York more, retired earlier, and spent more time seeing the world with Jon before he passed away. We put off so much, thinking that retirement was just around the corner and we'd have all the free time in the world to do all those things. But life and death don't work on the timetable we set for ourselves.

I learned that the hard way when so many of our dreams were taken from us when he died.

Our biggest dream was the Scottish cottage. How we came across it was pure luck, as neither of us had heard of the Isle of Murdina. Somehow, we ended up on the wrong ferry and found ourselves in the beautiful town of Port Ophelia. As soon as the colorful buildings on the main road came into view, my heart burst with excitement. Something about it felt right. I couldn't explain it if I tried.

As we wandered along the quaint streets that day, we discovered the cottage. Back then, it needed some work, but we could see its potential. We knew this would be a wonderful retirement home to escape to during those brutal summers in the South.

When most people think of retirement as the start of the end, we saw the potential of our future in that home. A new life.

Perhaps I got caught up in the stone walls, welcoming hearth, wild flowers, and views of the sunset from the patio. I could imagine all the lives that had lived there before and believed the house provided the warmth and support those families needed to thrive. I also thought it would do the same for us.

Unfortunately, we never got to see that for ourselves. But maybe you can.

I know I'm not imparting a turnkey house for you. It's miles from home and your life. I'm sure the house has fallen into even more disrepair these past few years. Regardless, if anyone can find the magic in this place, I know it's you.

I trust you'll see all this house represents: new beginnings, dreams realized, hope, and love. Even if you only get to visit it once because you decide to sell it or can only travel there every so often, if you choose to keep it, the feeling it provides will stay with you so you can find the courage to take on whatever's next in your life.

I love you, my Charlie girl.

Love,
Aunt Violet

Tears filled Charlie's eyes. How was it that her aunt, even after death, knew the right thing to say just when she needed it? There was a lot on the horizon for Charlie, and although her aunt wouldn't be there to give these words of encouragement along the way, she hoped whatever magic Aunt Violet had found in the cottage would make itself known tomorrow.

CHAPTER FOUR

To say Lachlan Hart was furious was an understatement. It wasn't like Charlie to blatantly ignore him. Sure, there were occasions during the weekend when she might take a little longer to call him back, but during the workweek? Never.

And she definitely wouldn't have missed the meeting she was so insistent on having last Friday. When Lachlan had finally emerged from his office after getting held up on another mind-numbing conference call, she was nowhere to be found. Annoyed, he had stalked back to his office and waited for a few minutes, only to realize she wasn't coming.

The question was why.

When he had asked around, one of the engineers said he had seen her race out of the office, looking like she'd been in rough shape. Lachlan assumed she had come down with something, even though she seemed perfectly fine only hours before. And if she was going to bail on her work and her *"important"* meeting with him, she would have done the responsible thing and told him.

She'd never leave him hanging. His time was valuable, and she knew it.

But as five days had come to pass, she'd gone radio silent. He would have known if it were something life-threatening, wouldn't he?

Lachlan punched the elevator button to the sixteenth floor, resisting the urge to tap his foot impatiently on the polished lobby floors. He cracked a knuckle and his neck. It had been a hell of a few days, first traveling to San Francisco to speak with more investors, followed by a client visit in Denver. It had been a total shit storm, but he sucked it up because it was for the betterment of his business.

Within the next three years, the cash infusion from these VC firms would nearly double MindThrive, an already impressive eight-hundred-person company. Although he'd rather stick his head through a fucking meat grinder than act like a prized show pony for the investors, he dealt with it. If going to these meetings meant he could hire the talent needed to take his company to the next level, so be it.

During his week of travel, he had emailed, called, and texted Charlie repeatedly to no avail. His inbox, which she usually managed, was a disaster. It overflowed to the point where he wanted to delete everything and start over. His voice mail wasn't much better.

He was frazzled, something he hadn't been in a long time. After Matteo's accident, Lachlan was thrust into the role of scaling the company to new heights.

Alone.

And as energizing as it was to watch a whole company emerge from the single algorithm he and Matteo had written a few years ago, it was hell doing it on his own. Without Matteo to help divide and conquer, Lachlan was quickly losing his footing in this delicate balancing act. He not only missed a deadline for one investor, but he was late to the client meeting because he couldn't find the address.

Charlie was always readily available to remind him of his schedule and handle the tedious details so he could go about his workweek with ease. Her absence threw him off his game, and now he wanted answers.

The elevator dinged as he reached the top floor. He stepped off and stalked purposefully through the office, heading straight to Charlie's desk to find out what the hell had gotten into her. It wasn't like her to go MIA and let work suffer.

But she wasn't there when he reached her desk. In her place sat a young, curly-haired brunette.

"Good morning, Mr. Hart." She had the perk of a high school cheerleader, which only grated on his nerves.

"Who the hell are you?" he asked gruffly.

Her cheery smile disappeared as her big blue eyes misted. "I...I'm your temp. Maddie."

Lachlan towered over the desk and stared down, his gaze boring into hers. He could have sworn her bottom lip quivered.

God, I'm an asshole.

He softened his approach. "I don't understand," he said calmly, his eyes still narrowed.

"I'm filling in for Charlie." The tears in her eyes had disappeared, but her look of terror remained.

He couldn't blame her. In the past, he'd been told he was intimidating, but he had to be a shark in this line of business. The tech arena was competitive. Those working in this space couldn't be soft and expect to survive. He learned that the hard way very quickly.

He wouldn't make that mistake again.

"Where's Charlie?" His patience had already worn dangerously thin.

"I don't know." She shrugged. "Not here anymore."

"Not here?" Lachlan's tone was a low growl, causing the girl to push back in her chair as if he were a rabid dog about to bite. Letting out a breath, he closed his eyes and pinched the bridge of his nose, trying to rein in his anger. "Start from the beginning."

She gave another unsure shrug. "There's not much to tell. The HR manager got me from a temp agency. I'm filling in for the next couple of weeks." As if sensing his anger, she quickly added, "I'm sorry I haven't gotten to your inbox and voice mail. IT still has to give me access. I had to sign an NDA and everything." She tentatively handed him a sheet of paper. "Also, I found this under Charlie's desk."

Lachlan snatched the paper from her and read the typed letter.

Lachlan,

This is my official resignation. My last day will be September twenty-first.

It's been a wonderful opportunity to work for MindThrive AI and for you personally these last three years. You've taught me so many valuable lessons, and it's exposed me to the possibilities for my future. At this time, I'll be pursuing a new career path. I hope we have a chance to work together again in a different capacity.

Thank you,
Charlie Middleton

Lachlan stared at the letter a moment longer. "She quit?" he whispered to himself in disbelief.

"Seems so," Maddie answered helpfully, her chipper personality now back.

His gaze snapped to her, making her squirm in her chair. "Get Devonny up here. Now!" He stalked to his office, pacing while he waited.

Gone.

His stomach clenched. Taking a seat at his desk, he rubbed his temples. This was a crucial time for the company. How could she have left knowing that? Knowing that he *needed* her to make this work?

Moments later, Devonny appeared, pulling him from his racing thoughts. She leaned her hip against the doorframe, crossing her arms. "Welcome back."

Lachlan crooked a finger, gesturing for her to come in. "Close the door behind you. Sit."

By the look on Devonny's face, she clearly didn't appreciate being ordered around, but she did as he asked. He had to give it to her; she wasn't often intimidated by him, which he respected. To have a successful business, he needed strong, smart people. Meek wouldn't work.

Speaking of which, Maddie needed to go.

"You wanted to see me?" she asked.

Lachlan slid Charlie's resignation across his desk and steepled his fingers together, waiting for Devonny's reaction. She scanned the letter, looking unsurprised.

"Yeah. I helped her write this. I know."

"And you didn't think to tell me?"

She cocked her head, a disapproving look crossing her features. "I tried. Since you were traveling, I left you emails and voice mails about it. I also sent you calendar invites for several interviews lined up next week." Despite her defensive posture, her voice stayed even.

"Charlie manages all of that for me," he shot back.

She let out a dry laugh. "She *really* did do everything for you." Devonny matched his sharp gaze. "You honestly never check your own messages?"

Was that judgment in her voice?

"Only after Charlie weeds out the crap."

Running a hand through her thick, dark hair, she let out a loud sigh. "Charlie intended on giving you the standard two-weeks, but a family emergency came up."

Lachlan snorted. "Family emergency. Yeah, just like all the assistants before. One day they're here, the next they're replaced. I've never had an assistant give me their full two-weeks."

Devonny shot a look that said, *Yeah, doesn't that tell you something?* "It's the truth. Her aunt passed away unexpectedly."

That sobered him. "Her aunt?"

"Violet. She helped raise Charlie. She was basically a second mother to her. Charlie went home to help her mom sort things out."

Lachlan nodded, absorbing the information. A wake and funeral would only take a few days, tops. Wouldn't she be back by now to finish her time?

"She hasn't answered any of my calls or texts." Surely she had her cell on her. Why wouldn't she have sent him a text to let him know she'd be indisposed?

"Charlie handed in her work phone last Friday when she left. She officially resigned effective September seventh."

The Friday she'd disappeared.

If his life could go into shambles in a matter of days without her, how was he going to survive while waiting to find a replacement to ramp up? Not only did he have major client deals in the works, but he also had a huge investor meeting in the next few days, one that could take MindThrive to the next level. He needed to concentrate and prepare. He couldn't do that with people like Maddie acting as his gatekeeper. She didn't have what it took. That was clear.

He needed Charlie. And fast.

"Where is she now?" he asked, mentally formulating a plan to bring her back.

"Scotland."

He shook his head with confusion. "Scotland? I thought she was from somewhere in the South."

"Her aunt left her a property in the will. Charlie had a few weeks to scope it out before her new gig so she can figure out what she wants to do with it."

Lachlan leaned forward, the wheels in his mind working. "Where?"

Devonny shrugged. "I can't remember off the top of my head. I'll check my texts when I return to my desk and send you the info." She stood to leave but paused. Her eyes narrowed. "Wait. Why do you want to know?"

He raised his chin with determination. "I'm going to bring her back."

"Lachlan, that's not going to—"

He held up a hand, cutting her off.

She pursed her lips.

"I'm going to Scotland to persuade her to rescind her resignation."

Devonny's mouth twitched as if she were trying to stop herself from laughing. "Okay," she said with patronizing amusement. "If you think you can convince her, then I'll send you the information."

"I do." His tone came out more juvenile than he'd intended.

"All right," she said in a singsong voice and wandered out of his office.

In the distance, he could have sworn he heard her laughing.

CHAPTER FIVE

"I won't sugarcoat it, lass. The house doesnae look the same as yer photo." Kennedy handed the picture back to Charlie.

"I figured." Her shoulders sank with dejection.

After a jam-packed day in Edinburgh, Charlie made her way to the ports the following morning to meet the property manager. They boarded the ferry and sat in the enclosed section, staring out the bow's large windows and watching occasional sunbreaks transform the sinister water into a calming deep blue.

Charlie gave Kennedy a quick glance from the corner of her eye and concluded he was one hundred percent Scottish male. Tall and brawny with a square jaw covered by a thick beard, blue eyes, and dark auburn hair, he could give Jamie Fraser a run for his money. His stylish hair and beard gave him an almost "lumbersexual" vibe, but she could tell he was the type who would roll up his sleeves and put in a day of hard work without complaint.

In the hour that Charlie had known him, she found him to be good-natured and easy to get along with. His humor and beaming smile put her at ease. And if she were honest, being around him caused a flurry of butterflies in her stomach, an almost foreign feeling for her. She'd been on some dates over the last couple of years, but nothing quite sparked her interest like Kennedy.

The feeling could simply be a reaction to being out of her element. With the free time, she could look up and take notice of what was around her. There were a lot of possibilities now, not just on the job front, but in life in general.

Maybe for once she could date a guy and not have to convince him that she and Lachlan *weren't* sleeping together, even if his constant texts and calls made it seem otherwise.

"I wouldn't worry yerself too much. Whit's fur ye'll no go past ye."

She knitted her eyebrows. "Um, what?"

He gave a deep laugh that rumbled his barreled-chest. "It means whatever is goin' tae happen tae ye, will happen. Just take it as it comes." His baritone voice held more of a Northern English accent. However, the Scottish came out every so often.

She relaxed back into her seat. "I guess you're right. I'll have to see it for myself and make the decision."

He nodded to the window. "We're just about there."

Charlie wandered to the front of the ferry to get a better look as the island's coast appeared in the distance. A faint unidentifiable outline on the horizon grew in size. She peered out the window, squinting to adjust her eyes against the harsh reflection of the sun bouncing off the water.

As the boat pushed forward, spots of colorful buildings emerged: deep corals, vibrant blues, seafoam greens, bright lavenders, and cheery yellows. It contrasted beautifully against the gray, stony cliff they were perched upon above the sea.

Her jaw dropped as the island became clearer. "It's adorable."

A range of cottages and buildings sat above the main strip of the colorful buildings and the long wooden port. They were staggered on small ascending hills, all beautifully constructed with stonework. From where Charlie stood, she could see billowing smoke from a few of their chimneys. Beyond the small village, mountains jutted up in the distance.

"Aye, many photographers come here. The village is bonny, but it's the landscapes on the farther side the island that draw 'em here. Many o' the areas are inhabited. Untouched."

Pressing her face harder against the glass like an awestruck child, she tried to get a better view. "What's out there?"

"A bit o' everything. Thick forests, mountains, cliffy beaches, clear lakes. In the warmer months, the purple heather sprouts across the mountains. So much o' it. I ne'er seen anything quite like it."

She turned to him with a hopeful grin. "Will I have a chance to see any of it?"

He shook his head. "Nae. With the winter approaching, they close the roads leading from the village. It gets too dangerous."

She cocked her head. "What do you mean?"

"The winter months bring strong gales. Some more than one-hundred-eighty kilometers per hour. Most villagers leave in November and return in March."

"How do they make any money? A whole town leaves? What about their jobs?"

Kennedy nodded. "They do well in the months here. Fishing, tourism, and even whisky. Most have smaller homes in places like Glasgow and the surrounding towns during the winter. Family homes."

"I see."

Kennedy reached for Charlie's hand, causing a jolt to shoot up her arm. She tried to hide her reaction. "Ye might want tae sit. We're pulling intae the port. It can get bumpy."

Charlie took a seat next to him, sliding into his hard frame when the ferry bounced from side-to-side as it pulled into port. Kennedy laughed and wrapped a strong arm across her shoulders to keep her steady.

As the engines died down and the captain gave the all clear, he stood and offered a hand. Charlie took it, smiling. In New York, she was lucky if a guy even thought to hold a door for her. Those men were definitely not raised like the boys in the South or Scotland.

"Are ye ready tae see yer cottage?"

Excitement swelled inside her, shooing away the fogginess of her old, boring life. She remembered what her aunt had said in the letter, making her eager to see the magical place that was so special to her and her uncle.

"Yes!" She squeezed his hand and nearly dragged him down the dock.

But a few minutes later, and a tough trek up the steep hill, showed her that words and photos don't always paint the right picture. After making their way through the cute main street and taking the stone stairs that led to the road up the hill, Charlie stood in front of a structure that had seen better days.

"Are you sure this is it?" Her voice was deflated.

Kennedy flashed a smile that made her feel a little less disappointed. "It's nae as bad as it seems."

She glanced at the picture in her hand and lifted her gaze to the cottage in front of her. The front yard was overgrown with tall grass and dying wild flowers. The stone fence circling the property was starting to crumble, and the iron gate had fallen off. From what she could tell, there were two broken windows in the front, and the roof looked like it was seconds away from caving in. How it would survive the crazy winter winds was beyond her.

"The roof?"

He gave a nod. "Aye. Nae verra guid. I inspected everything before yer arrival. The roof needs tae be replaced first. The door in the back is rotted. Some animals had gotten in through the windows. I boarded them up for ye."

"And the animals?" she asked with raised eyebrows.

"I got them all." He paused. "I think."

"Kennedy..."

"Dinna worry. A guid muckin will set it right." He elbowed her playfully.

"Muckin?"

He rolled his eyes. "A cleaning," he answered in a mock New York accent. "How you doin'," he added in his best Joey Tribbiani impression, wagging his eyebrows suggestively.

Charlie giggled and elbowed him back at the attempt. "Good try, but you know I'm from the South. We don't sound like that."

He fanned eyes eyelashes and placed the back of his hand to his forehead dramatically. "'As God as my witness,'" he drawled.

She erupted into more laughter, something she hadn't done since the news of her aunt's passing. "Wouldn't take you for a *Gone with the Wind* fan."

"Canna a big, tough, burly Scot be cultured, aye?"

She held up her hands in mock surrender. "I stand corrected. I shouldn't have been so quick to assume."

"With me, lass, ye get both brawn *and* brains. My mither raised me tae be quite the gentleman too."

She crossed her arms and tilted her head. "Is that so?"

"Aye. For example, I'll help ye get the house sorted for the storm."

She dropped her arms, all joking aside. "Storm? What storm?"

"Ye have nae heard of it? Scotland doesnae get much for storms, maybe every decade or so. But one is bound tae strike in a few days. Most people have already packed up tae leave for the winter. Only the essential stores have been left open so the town's fowk can secure their homes."

Charlie eyed the cottage with its broken door and saggy roof. "You think this will withstand the storm?"

He shrugged his broad shoulders. "I dinna ken. It's lasted this long somehow. Let's go intae town tae get supplies."

The two of them walked in companionable silence down the stairs to the main road. There, Charlie was tossed about by the people rushing around from the small stores, hands full of wood and sandbags.

"When's this storm supposed to come?" she asked, ducking out of the way when a man carrying wood swung past her.

Kennedy grabbed her arm, pulling her out of harm's way. "Couple o' days. Last ferry will be tomorrow evening. I'll help ye get yer house set before we have tae evacuate the island."

Charlie scanned the various stores housed in colorful buildings along the coast. A bar, cafe, restaurant, hardware store, bait store, grocer, butcher, pharmacy, and B&B were lining one side. Some had been boarded up with signs saying they'd return in the spring.

Charlie nodded toward the grocer. "Mind if I get some groceries? Looks like they're still open." She paused in thought. "Hey, how are we supposed to bring all these supplies up the hill?" She had been winded walking up the steep stairs to the village above, even with Kennedy carrying her bags. She would probably die if she had to carry up groceries and storm preparations.

"Do nae worry, lass. I will rent a truck from the hardware store."

"Great. I'll meet you over there."

Charlie entered the small store, finding it still well stocked despite the mass exodus of the island. She grabbed a cart and perused the tight aisles.

"Allo, lassie. Welcome. Everything's half off," an older man with a maroon apron called out from the end of the aisle and gave a warm, toothy smile.

"Thank you." She scanned the shelves near her. "Do you have any bottles of water?"

"Sure do. Aisle three." He pointed to the left. "Are ye new here? Yer accent. American?"

Charlie grinned and nodded, pushing a small cart toward him so they weren't yelling across the store. "Yeah. It's my first time here. My aunt and uncle have—had...*had*—a home on Queen Mary's Alley."

"Aye. Violet and Jon?"

Charlie's heart squeezed. "You knew them?"

"Only Americans I kenned of on that road." He raised a hand and scratched at the thinning silver hair on his head. "I have nae seen them in some time. How are they?"

Her eyes misted, but she blinked it away. "They've passed away."

He gave a sad shake of his head, his mouth downturned. "Such a shame. Wonderful people they were."

"They were the best."

"Sorry for yer loss, lassie. My name is Callum. Pleased tae meet yer acquaintance." He held out his hand. Charlie took it, noting the rough calluses on his palm—the palm of a working man, something she hadn't felt while living in New York. "Please take as much as ye need. I'll be shutting down the shop tonight and taking what I can. No sense in things going tae waste."

"Thanks, I will."

As he turned to go, he stopped in his tracks. "By the way, have ye seen a dog wandering about?"

Charlie's eyebrows furrowed. "I'm sorry?"

Callum slipped a hand into the front pocket of his smock, pulling out a flyer for a missing dog. "Me dog. She chased after a rabbit yesterday and has nae returned." The lines in his face twisted with worry, tugging at Charlie's heart.

She took the flyer and inspected the photo of a beautiful retriever. "I'm sorry. I haven't seen her." She handed him the paper, but he pushed it back, wrapping her hand around it tightly.

"Please," he pleaded, "if ye see her during yer time on the island, call the number on the flyer. We will be taking the last ferry tomorrow. I dinnae want tae leave her behind." His voice cracked, causing a pang in Charlie.

"I will absolutely call if I see her," she promised.

His smile was warm and grateful. "Thank ye, lassie."

A few minutes later, Charlie stumbled under the bulkiness of her grocery bags and into the hardware store. She spotted Kennedy's large, broad frame in the back almost instantly.

"Wow. Did ye buy the whole store?" he commented when he saw the amount of bags she carried. "That's a lot o' food for a night."

She waddled to where he was and placed the bags on the ground. "I can always take some back to the mainland."

Kennedy hooked his index finger through the handle of one of the bags and peeked in. "Nothing perishable, aye? There's a small refrigerator in the cottage kitchen, but I fear the electricity can be fickle. Would nae want all this tae go tae waste."

"I wasn't sure if there was a fridge, so I limited the perishable purchases."

He nodded. "Guid. Almost done here. Waiting for the keys tae the truck."

Charlie leaned against the register counter casually as they waited. "So how will this work?"

"Sorry?"

"You said you're going to help me get the house together. Are you staying on the island tonight too?"

He shook his head. "Nay. I'll be taking the last ferry out tonight and will return in the morn' for last minute stuff. First order o' business is tae get the back door fixed." He eyed her warily. "Are ye okay on yer own tonight or will ye return tae Glasgow with me?"

"I'm going to stay. Staying the night might give me a better idea of the condition of the cottage and what decision I should make. Since the storm is cutting into the time I had planned on spending here, I need to make the most of it."

"Och aye. I understand."

A half an hour later, they got the keys to the truck and the supplies loaded. They took a steep, narrow road back to the residential neighborhood and brought everything inside. As Kennedy took in the last of the supplies from the hardware store, Charlie used the time to explore the house. It wasn't large by any means, but it was cozy.

She circled the open space of the first floor, likely used for the living room and the dining area. The walls were exposed stone, the same as the outside. The floors were made with beautiful, large planked pine. However, her favorite part of the room was the huge stone hearth in the center. It was welcoming and homey, and she could see why her aunt and uncle had fallen in love with it nearly a decade before. She could imagine them there in the fall when the weather had turned crisp, enjoying a steaming cup of tea and a good book, warmed by the fireplace.

Trailing her fingers along the dusty live-edge mantel, she stopped to grasp a single picture frame resting on it. It was the same one she had on her desk from her college graduation six years ago. Charlie was in a graduation robe, Aunt Violet, Uncle Jon, and her mother surrounded her as they all beamed at the camera.

She sighed. This was the last photo of all of them together before her uncle had died the following year. She traced a finger along the happy faces, remembering how loved she felt that day.

Once she'd placed the photo down carefully, she continued to explore the first floor. A half bathroom, a broom closet, and a kitchen with a two-person table. She took the stairs to the second floor, finding two bedrooms, each with a stripped bed and basic nightstand. Charlie wandered down the hall, locating a full bathroom with a gorgeous claw-foot tub.

Despite the disrepair, Charlie could understand why her aunt Violet had said it was special. The cottage was simple, with the hint of history hidden in its walls.

After living in "the city that never sleeps" with its constant noise, Charlie found the silence here refreshing. She thought the remoteness of the island would make her feel disconnected, but something about it felt good. Right. During her initial walk-through, she knew she wanted to hold on to the home if she could.

But would the cost of the repairs even be feasible?

Their trip to the hardware store had added up quickly, and they only purchased bare necessities to hopefully preserve the home while the storm passed through. She could only imagine how expensive it would be to get the plumbing and electrical up to the twenty-first century, let alone the price to repair the roof.

Sure, she could hold on to the home through the winter and save funds for when she could start repairs come spring, but that depended on if she landed a good paying job right after the bootcamp. Would a few months of saving make a dent in the budget needed to get this place where it needed to be?

After making her way downstairs, Charlie busied herself by making a simple dinner while Kennedy replaced the decayed back door, complete with a sturdy lock.

Every so often, Charlie sneaked a glance at him. Truthfully, seeing Kennedy use his strength to pull off the creaky door was kind of hot. The way his large hands took control of the splintered wood, forcefully ripping off the door, and how his hair flopped over his forehead with each tug gave her a thrill.

Watching a capable man do manual labor was a turn-on. It was so different from the world she knew back in New York.

She gave herself a mental shake. She needed to keep her cool. Keep it professional.

A dalliance with someone who lived on a whole other continent wasn't ideal, even *if* she was the type to do that.

At least in New York, a one-night stand had a possibility of turning into something more. That idea made her feel less guilty about hookups that fizzled out before they began. A hookup with a guy from Scotland was almost guaranteed to be a onetime thing.

Or would it? What if she were to keep the cottage?

Oh my God, get a grip, Charlie. You see one friendly, good-looking guy, and you're already considering what would happen if you hooked up. Chill out. He's just doing his job. If the house blows away, he loses a client.

Just as she convinced herself to let it go, Kennedy stopped pounding at the door and looked up at her. Their eyes locked, and he gave her a slow, panty-dropping smile.

Oh boy. This is going to be a long night.

CHAPTER SIX

HER NIGHT alone in the cottage had been surprisingly restful. Charlie thought the absence of car horns, sirens, and the occasional neighbor playing music way too loud late on a work night would be jarring. Despite that, and the fact that she was sleeping in a completely foreign place altogether, she'd slept soundly. The hoots of owls and chirps of night bugs had lulled her into a deep, comforting slumber.

She needed this. A night of uninterrupted sleep without worrying about her mother or Lachlan waking her up. Even when he hadn't called her, she had found herself jumping awake, scared she'd missed a message from him.

Maybe she had a little PTSD from all of that.

The next morning, she took a shower, quickly learning the hot water lasted all of two minutes. As the cold water shocked her, she powered through as fast as she could. After that unexpected wake-up call, she sat at the kitchen table with a cup of tea and a danish from the grocery store, embracing the comfort of the old home and its peaceful solitude. She even found its occasional creaks and groans to be charming.

And then there was last night with Kennedy. He was a breath of fresh air. Despite her attraction to him, she kept things light and friendly. They shared dinner together—a plate of spaghetti with a side of crusty bread. Kennedy had a way of putting her at ease with his engaging stories and hearty laugh. She couldn't help but laugh with him when his deep chuckle filled the air.

It was nice to have a normal, stress-free dinner with a man. Although she hadn't had a boyfriend in a few years—once again, thanks to Lachlan and his inability to let her have a freaking moment to herself—she tried to go on a date every so often.

Sure, she'd met some duds through the dating apps, but she'd also met some decent men too. None of them, however, had a calming effect like Kennedy. In a city that was full of people who were hungry to grow their careers and material wealth, finding someone down-to-earth and humble was hard to come by.

Charlie was also passionate about building her career—especially now that she had a focus—but she was still a strong believer in work-life balance. Why it took her so long to quit Lachlan was beyond her. Working for him went against everything she stood for. It compromised time for herself, her friends, and her loved ones, making it hard to remember who she was and what she wanted.

She wouldn't let that happen again. She would stand firmly behind that.

Coming to Scotland shed a blinding light on everything she had pushed aside. She vowed to make sure she didn't fall into those same bad habits when she got back to New York and started her new career.

A sound at the front door pulled Charlie from her thoughts. She padded barefoot along the hardwood floor, tea in hand, and opened the door. On the front step, Kennedy leaned against the doorjamb with a charming grin spread across his face.

"Morning."

God. Will I ever get tired of that accent?

She opened the door wider, allowing his broad frame to squeeze through. "Good morning."

"How did ye sleep?" He crossed the threshold and placed his toolbox on the kitchen counter, stopping short at the sight of the open danish box. He snagged a piece for himself, nearly inhaling it in one bite.

"By all means, help yourself." Charlie laughed as she followed him to the kitchen. "Surprisingly good. Tea? Coffee?" She held up an empty mug.

He shook a head and leaned against the counter casually. "Nae. Had coffee on the way over."

"What do we have on the agenda today?" she asked as she took her seat at the table to finish her breakfast.

"I want tae poke around the roof and see what we're working with. Also, add a few more boards tae the broken windows and shutter up the others in case of debris. I'll try tae get as much done as I can, but I'm afraid I'll be leaving ye a little sooner than expected."

She stopped picking at the danish. "What do you mean?"

"I have some business tae attend tae in Glasgow this afternoon. I'll be taking the noon ferry back."

"I see."

She tried not to let her disappointment show. She was enjoying his company way too much and somehow convinced herself that if a kiss happened, it wouldn't be all that bad. A kiss was harmless, right?

"I ken I do nae need tae remind ye, but ye must be on the last ferry tonight. Last one is at five."

She gave him a thumbs-up and shoved the last of the pastry in her mouth. "You got it. I already packed my bags. I'll be ready. I might take an earlier one anyway."

"Aye. Guid idea." He pushed off the counter. "Let's get tae work."

* * *

Charlie and Kennedy spent the next few hours getting the house situated, and she had to admit she'd never had so much fun doing manual labor. Even though their tasks were exhausting, from holding up heavy boards for the windows to crawling through the dusty attic to check the roof, Kennedy had a way of making it entertaining.

Maybe it was his humor. Or perhaps it was the smoldering glances he'd toss her way. Or the way his hand would graze hers as he positioned the wood planks for the windows. Each look or touch sent a thrill through her.

There was a good chance none of this meant anything to him. Charlie was a little rusty in the flirting department, but she relished the appreciative way his gaze lingered on her all the same. She liked the attention. Being here with him eased the stress and sadness she felt on her way to Scotland only a couple days ago. Having that reprieve was a nice escape, even if only a temporary distraction.

It was nearly noon by the time they wrapped up. Kennedy was in the kitchen, packing the last of his tools.

"I hate that we dinnae have time tae board the upstairs windows, but I think it will hold." He gave a shrug. "There is nae much in the house tae damage if something gets through. Just a bit o' clean up."

"A good muckin', right?" She rolled her eyes and leaned against the doorjamb with her arms crossed. "I guess we'll add that to the growing list of to-dos for this house."

"Hopefully the roof doesnae blow off," he half joked. Then again, the roof was questionable. They definitely had noticed areas where rainwater had gotten in when they had inspected it earlier. She just hoped those sections could be repaired and she wouldn't need to replace the whole thing.

Kennedy tossed her a set of keys, which Charlie fumbled. She picked them off the floor as gracefully as she could.

"Ye will take the truck back tae the store, aye? Will be easier tae get yer luggage down the hill with it."

"Sure. What time does he close?"

"He'll be taking the three o'clock ferry. There's a mail slot where ye can slip the keys in if he's gone." He gave her a serious look. "Please, do nae forget—"

"The last ferry is at five," she said for him. "Got it. If I could keep a tech mogul on track for three years with his insane schedule, I think I can remember this one thing."

A wide smile lifted on his lips, and he held up his hands defensively. "All right. Foolish o' me tae assume a lass cannae take care o' herself."

"That's right," she said, puffing out her chest.

Kennedy walked to the front door and swung it open. He turned back and added, "I will give ye a call in a couple o' days and show ye around Glasgow."

Charlie grinned. "Sounds perfect. Safe travels."

She watched him walk to the stairs that led to the main road before closing the door behind her. Feeling gritty and dirty from a day of labor, she took another quick shower and slipped into a pair of fitted jeans and a casual T-shirt and made her way outside. She wanted to take a walk before she left to get a feel for the island and make the most of her limited time here.

The wind blowing from the east made the air balmy, unusual for September in Scotland, or so she was told. The sun danced behind the occasional cloud, almost making her believe there wasn't a storm threatening to flatten the island town. However, the shuttered homes and postapocalyptic lack of people reminded her not to get too comfortable.

Charlie walked farther up the hill, enjoying the lovely cottages along the road. Each house was similar in structure, but the owner made it their own. Some had lush gardens with large fountains for the birds. Others gave their homes a pop of color, choosing decorative shutters, doors, and roofs. Some houses had painted the exterior stone in white, aqua, or lavender, much like the buildings down by the port.

As Charlie wandered the street, she wondered what it was like during the height of the season. Were the neighbors friendly? Did the main road buzz with activity? Did people come by the boatload to visit? Would they have festivals and fish fries? Or was it quiet like this?

Abandoned. Boarded up. Forgotten.

In the distance, the ferry's faint horn floated through the thick air. Charlie checked the time. She had a couple more hours to explore before she needed to go.

Only a couple more hours to discover the same specialness of this place her dear aunt Violet had.

Still torn about whether to keep or sell the cottage, Charlie hoped her time here would help her decide the fate of her Scottish home.

CHAPTER SEVEN

LACHLAN STRETCHED, his knees hitting the seat in front of him, as he massaged the kink out of his neck. His lower back was killing him, and his left foot had gone numb.

He hadn't flown coach in years, but unfortunately for him, last-minute tickets to London meant he was shit out of luck. He had hoped to sleep on the overnight flight from New York, but the tiny seats made it impossible for him to settle comfortably. Not to mention, the broad-shouldered guy next to him forced Lachlan to lean to one side to make space.

That was, only after a silent battle for the arm rest. Rarely one to lose, Lachlan's pride stung when the dude inserted his dominance, not willing to budge once he staked his claim.

How did airlines expect people to travel like this? Crammed in their seats with only stale crackers or peanuts to survive off of? Prisoners had more luxuries than coach.

After a slow and frustrating deplaning, he stood in the middle of Heathrow. Rubbing his eyes, he searched for a coffee stand in the busy airport. Finally, he spotted one with only a moderate line.

"Mornin', sir. How might I help you?" A young woman with a

thick Welsh accent and a wide smile greeted him when he approached the counter. She scanned him up and down—he assumed she meant to be discreet but failed—as he studied the menu. He caught her blue eyes ogling him at the last second, causing her to look down and blush.

"I'll take a Red Eye, please."

"Right away." She scurried to the coffee machine to make his caffeine-heavy drink and slid it to him without making eye contact. He sighed, feeling bad he embarrassed her.

He handed her the money with a large tip and grabbed the paper cup. "Thanks."

Taking his coffee, he made his way to ground transportation, scanning the area for his driver. After a moment of looking, he found a gray-haired gentleman in a black blazer holding a sign that said "Hart." Lachlan raised a hand to get his attention and navigated the crowd to meet him.

"I'm Lachlan Hart." He offered his free hand.

The driver took it and shook it with enthusiasm, nearly causing the coffee cup to slip from Lachlan's other hand. "Hi there. I'm Benjamin, sir. I'll be taking you to Glasgow, right?"

For a large, older man, Lachlan had expected a more distinguished voice. Benjamin, however, sounded like a spirited teen.

"Yeah. How long will that take?" Lachlan checked his Rolex. Barely six in the morning local time. The dark sky outside made it feel like midnight.

"Just under seven hours, sir."

Lachlan stifled a groan. He had tried to book a connecting flight to Glasgow, but learned all inbound flights were grounded due to an unprecedented storm predicted to hit the area in the next couple of days.

Seven hours with a man who had too much energy for Lachlan to handle without proper sleep or an IV drip of caffeine was going to be torture. Hopefully, the guy would get a hint, and Lachlan could catch some shut-eye once they got out of the city and onto the soothing streets of the countryside.

"Sir?" Benjamin said, his eyes clouded with worry.

"You can call me Lachlan."

"Lachlan, sir. You still want me to take you to the Kennacraig port?"

"Yeah. Why?" Lachlan pulled his carry-on forward, trying to Benjamin to get moving. The driver grabbed the bags from him politely and led him to a black town car.

"The CalMac Ferry will be closing this evening. I believe the last ferry to the island is at four this afternoon to get the remaining folks who are preparing their homes."

"Because of the storm?"

Lachlan got Charlie's personal cell number from Devonny before he left, but it had been impossible to reach her. Either the call would fail or it would ring once and go to voice mail. Even though he'd left a couple of messages, he wasn't feeling particularly hopeful. All his sent text messages gave him a delivery error, so he doubted the voice mail would fare much better.

The man nodded. "They're expecting it to be quite destructive." He raised his eyebrows conspiratorially. "The Gulf Stream typically makes the weather mild, but climate change appears to be affecting our seas. People are nervous." They reached the town car, and Benjamin placed the bag in the trunk while Lachlan slipped into the back seat.

Lachlan swallowed a tennis ball–sized lump in his throat. *Is she worth all this trouble?*

Yes. After a week from hell without her, it was a resounding yes.

* * *

Later that afternoon, Lachlan sat on ferry leading to the Isle of Murdina, a small island off the coast of western Scotland. He took the forty-five-minute ferry ride as an opportunity to figure out what the hell he was even doing.

It was insane, really. He shook his head. *This must be some sort of psychotic break caused by disorder.*

That was it. His life was a mess without Charlie. Of course he would be desperate to get her back.

Lachlan looked out to the water, now choppy from the gusting wind. He was the only one taking the ferry and was glad for it. He'd been on one too many New York ferries during rough weather to know people couldn't hold down their breakfast.

He cringed at the thought.

Looking at the murky water, he was reminded of his childhood in the small coastal town of Monmouth Beach. Life had been easy in those days. All he had to worry about was shredding waves and chasing girls.

He suppressed a laugh. If anyone heard him speak like that, they'd think he'd lost it. Most people who knew him now wouldn't see any semblance of the beach bum surfer he once was.

That was a lifetime ago, and he wasn't the same carefree boy who soaked up the sun during the day and tinkered away on his computer at night. Now, it was up to him to keep the company growing. The innovations they were working on in the artificial intelligence space were astounding. Lachlan owed it to Matteo to see this through, for a number of reasons.

In the distance, he could see the outline of the island, the dense fog making it dark and sinister. A rogue wave splashed the front window, startling him.

He prayed Charlie was still there and that they could get back to the mainland quickly. Growing up, he had seen hurricanes ravage his hometown and didn't want to be stuck on an island with no inland escape.

He was taking a big risk for Charlie. Sure, she was just an assistant —a good one—but still. He couldn't figure out what it was about her that made him think traipsing across the Atlantic Ocean to some remote island was a good idea. He should be using this time to prepare for the investor meeting in New York in a couple of days—one that could take his company to places he and Matteo had only dreamed of a few years ago.

Maybe it was because his life felt like it was spinning out of control without Charlie there. For the past three years, it had been smooth sailing. He knew she was a great worker, but this last week showed him just how much he needed her.

But was that *really* enough for all of this?

He shuddered as he thought of the mess that was Maddie.

Before falling asleep in the town car earlier, Lachlan had tried to find some semblance of order in his life. He spent the first two hours of the ride trying to get a handle on his growing inbox before he gave up altogether. When that all-too-familiar pain shot behind his eyes, he decided to close his laptop, praying the temp would get access to his accounts soon to take care of it.

However, if he got his way, it would be Charlie taking care of it.

Charlie.

Maybe he should have shown his appreciation more often. Or he could have stopped relying on her so much so that weekends and nights could be hers alone. Would a raise or spot bonus help convince her to come back?

Doubtful.

Charlie wasn't money hungry like the rest of New York. Yet he had no idea what her drives were. With any deal, he researched the motivations of the other party. What did they want to walk away with? Once he figured that out, he would close them every time. He needed to apply that successful method with Charlie.

Lachlan sighed. He should have gotten to know her better. Without those details, he was flying blind. Usually confident in his power of persuasion, he worried he might not win this one.

All he knew was he would put up one hell of a fight. He wasn't leaving Scotland without her.

CHAPTER EIGHT

CHARLIE WANDERED BACK to the cottage after her neighborhood exploration, deciding she was going to do everything she could to keep this house. Aunt Violet and Uncle Jon had so many options for retirement—a whole world's worth. But something about this particular town on this specific island was the one that spoke to them.

It spoke to her too.

All through high school and college, Charlie had the privilege to travel a lot. She loved the opportunity to immerse herself in new places, acting as a spectator as she discovered more about the world and its different cultures. She treasured learning the history of places, the story of their people, their customs, and their myths and legends.

Travel was the one time she could step outside herself, her problems, and her unmet wants, and see there was so much more out there. More options. New things to discover. Other life paths to explore.

It made her feel unstuck.

She hadn't gone someplace new in longer than she cared to admit.

These last few years, travel had been scarce, only limited to the tri-state area and visiting her mother and aunt in Georgia.

"You're going to suffocate," Aunt Violet had said to her after two years of being bound to the United States.

Aunt Violet was similar to her, so passionate about seeing the world. Her mother—despite the upsetting history she had with her family in Georgia—was perfectly content staying local.

On occasion, she had visited Charlie in New York, but Charlie could tell she preferred the sunny, humid, slower way of life in the South. She laughed when she thought back to the horrified look on her mother's face when she saw a homeless man urinating in the subway station. No wonder her mother's visits had become sparser over the years.

There was a lot unknown about this cottage, such as if it would survive this storm and the cost of repairs. New York wasn't exactly cheap. It felt like it took forever to save the money for the bootcamp, and that was a fraction of what the repair costs could be.

There was also the issue of whether Charlie would land a job that could support her bills plus the added cost of the cottage. Would her new job give her the flexibility to travel back and forth?

She shook her head with resolve. This was the time in her life where she would take charge. Make decisions and stick with them. She would handle her life on her own terms. Like her career path, she was vowing to commit to the things that mattered to her and not let anything get in her way.

She deserved to be a little selfish for once. To put herself first.

Walking through the neighborhoods, full of winding roads and beautiful homes, gave her peace. This short walk had made her conclude she wouldn't give it up without trying.

She couldn't.

She wanted to do right by her aunt and uncle. She'd put in her best effort to keep the cottage and ensure whatever job she took wouldn't prevent her from coming here. Even if it didn't work out, she would know she tried. And she'd at least have some memories at the home before she had to let it go.

Charlie sang softly to herself as she entered the cottage and headed for the kitchen to collect the last of her things and the remaining food.

She checked her phone, still finding the service to be nonexistent. Thankfully, Kennedy let her use his phone to check in with her mother earlier in the day.

She had an hour to kill before the last ferry would leave. She planned to winterize the house per Kennedy's instructions, toss the bags into the truck, and drop it off at the hardware store on her way to the port. She ensured she'd have plenty of time to get to the dock so she wouldn't miss the last boat out.

A gust of wind rattled the boards on the windows, whistling through holes where the glass was broken. Charlie shivered at the eerie sound.

Her walk had been pleasant, for the most part. However, the distant clouds and occasional breeze reminded her not to get complacent. The village had turned into a ghost town these last few hours. Earlier that morning, she had watched the last of the island people milling about on the main road. By midafternoon, it was empty.

She wondered if she was the last one left. It sure felt like it.

Charlie lugged her suitcase down the stairs and made it outside. Rolling the bags along the bumpy path that was missing a few stones —another thing she had to fix—she walked through the gap where the iron gate used to be and stopped in front of the borrowed truck parked by the curb.

Popping the tailgate open, she hoisted the oversized bag into the truck bed. As she trudged back to the cottage to grab the food, a sound made her stop dead in her tracks.

Her blood went cold.

A voice called out her name.

A voice she knew all too well.

It couldn't be. There's no possible way.

She turned slowly, coming face-to-face with Lachlan Hart.

CHAPTER NINE

LACHLAN STUFFED the slip of paper with the address into his pocket and slowly wandered up the steep street, searching for the house numbers. He pulled off his suit jacket—now a wrinkled mess—and wiped a bead of sweat off his eyebrow. The cloud cover and blowing wind offered no relief from the sticky, humid air.

Benjamin had said the island was shutting down, but in Lachlan's experiences growing up on the coast, only half of the people actually adhered to the mandatory evacuation.

The Isle of Murdina was not the same.

The moment he stepped off the boat, he felt like he was transported to an abandoned town—like one of the mining communities that had fallen into disarray throughout the United States. The towns were all that remained of the crushed American Dream so many had strived to achieve, but never did.

Although the buildings here weren't shells of what they used to be, much like those ghost towns, the lack of people and shuttered windows made it feel all the same.

He pulled his phone from his pocket, wondering if Charlie had gotten back to him. He frowned when he saw no service bars. So much for the global plan he paid a fortune for. It was no use out here. Slipping his phone into his pocket, he made a mental note that the last ferry would arrive for passengers in an hour. He hoped he could locate the cottage well before then.

Lachlan shifted the carry-on duffel on his shoulder and continued up the hill. Despite his deeply regimented workout routine—a daily three-mile run and weight training four days a week—the incline burned his calves. As his stiff shoes bit into his heels, he considered that maybe his Italian leather shoes weren't the best choice for this impromptu hike.

He walked for another five uncomfortable minutes, noting the house numbers were getting closer to the one Devonny had scribbled down for him. If his calculations were right, the cottage should be just past the bend. As he made the turn, he saw the first and only person on this godforsaken island.

Her back was to him, but Lachlan would know that red hair anywhere.

"Charlie!" His deep voice bellowed through the silent streets, a jarring noise in the otherwise silence. He picked up momentum, eager to reach her.

"Char—" His voice caught in his throat. Her name died on his lips.

Charlie swung around at the exact moment a sunbreak cut through the clouds above, raining light down on her like she was some sort of angel. Her thick crimson hair shimmered like a dancing fire on a winter night. It cascaded in waves past her shoulders, leading to a simple T-shirt that strained against lush breasts. Curvy hips sat upon full legs in a tight pair of fitted jeans.

Her face was free of makeup, showing Lachlan fresh, unblemished skin aside from the faint smattering of freckles on her nose and cheeks. Her large emerald eyes—green like the open, rolling fields in the Scottish countryside—went wide. And in an instant, transformed into narrow slits, her cheeks taking on an attractive shade of pink.

Lachlan had been surrounded by beautiful women before,

especially after his success in the tech space. For special events, it wasn't unusual for him to have an acquaintance attend with him.

All of them were gorgeous and successful in their own right, and any man would feel lucky to have them on his arm. But for Lachlan, those events were just that: a social affair—maybe the occasional no-strings-attached sex—but that was as far as it would go.

Those willowy, poised beauties knew he couldn't offer them more. He didn't have the time. He was always upfront about that—before the sex, of course—but damn if they didn't hope.

Although his mother said he'd make the time and sacrifices for the right woman, none of them had ever been able to pull his interest away from work long enough to have him consider that as an option.

But something about seeing Charlie in front of him now made him pause in a way those women never could. He was never caught off guard. Never shaken to the core. But she had him feeling like he had been the world's biggest idiot for missing a woman like her. A woman who had been practically attached to his side for three years.

Could he really have been that blind?

He cleared his throat, attempting to gather his composure, hoping she didn't catch that he'd been staring at her wordlessly for the last minute. He tried to convince himself it was simply the shock of seeing her in a different environment. In all the years he had known her, he'd never seen her so...casual. Free.

Real.

He had always thought of her as the "girl next door," with a certain innocence and professionalism to her. But nothing about this version of girl next door was innocent. The way she glared at him and how she stood there as if ready for battle intrigued him.

Something about the way she looked at him was raw. Honest. For a moment, he saw a part of her she had always hidden behind being the perfect assistant.

And now he wanted to know more.

So much more.

He preferred this Charlie. This Charlie was touchable.

And as he closed the distance between them, he almost did just that. He wanted to feel the smooth skin of her cheek. To run his finger over her plush lips. To inhale her scent—a mix of jasmine and pepper. Floral and clean without being overwhelming.

"What the hell are you doing here, Lachlan?" Her tone was low and angry, making her faint Southern accent more pronounced. It wavered when she said his name, as if she were trying to reel in her anger.

"I came to find you."

She threw her hands in the air and let out a frustrated noise. "You can't even let me resign in peace, can you? You just have to infiltrate my life. Fill every moment with you."

Lachlan's cock twitched at the thought of filling her.

Was he in some sort of *Twilight Zone*? It wasn't like him to react to something so innocent.

Get your head out of the gutter and in the game, man. You're a problem solver. Put your dick's needs on the back burner and focus on why you're here: convincing her to come back.

"That's not—"

"I came here to grieve my aunt. I needed to take care of a family matter. Not that I need to explain that to you. I don't work for you anymore!"

She stalked back to the house and swung the door open, disappearing inside. Lachlan, against his better judgment, went in after her.

For once, his mind was no longer in control. His actions were driven by pure primal need, one only Charlie could fill. A need he never known he'd had.

Lachlan shook his head, trying to kick-start his brain again. He couldn't persuade her to come back to work if his idiotic heart was penning Shakespearean sonnets about how her mere presence made his knees weak and turned him inside out.

It made no sense, this sudden switch, but curiosity got the best of him.

He wandered through the small open space of the living area, following the sound of shuffling and quiet cursing to the kitchen. Charlie stuffed boxes of food and fruit into reusable grocery bags, her body tensing when he entered the room.

Sighing, she closed her eyes before standing up to address him. She crossed her arms. "Why, Lachlan? You shouldn't even be here. You have the investor meeting tomorrow."

He jabbed his index finger in the air to emphasize the point she just made. "See. That's why I'm here. I need you, Charlie. My work-life has been a disaster without you."

She blinked at him, her expression one of disbelief. "Seriously? You came to a remote island in Scotland because you can't handle finding a replacement for me?" She raised her eyebrows. "And the fact that you mentioned work-life as if it were one and the same is a whole other problem I'm not even going to touch."

"This is a crucial time for the company. You know that. I need someone I can count on to keep me on my game."

She dropped her arms and let out a huff. "You can't put that pressure on me. Of course I know it's an important time for the company. I was there every step of the way to prepare for it."

"So wouldn't you want to see that through?" He was a bastard for exploiting her unshakable work ethic, but he was bordering desperation. All reasonable strategies he had to convince her to come back were falling apart. He hadn't expected her to be so candid or vocal. It was a side he'd never seen of her, and there was no way he could have prepared for that.

"MindThrive is *your* company. Not mine. You're a big boy. You can figure it out."

Lachlan stood there for a moment, processing the disdain in her voice. Charlie had never spoken out of line. Most conversations with her were short and pleasant, her voice steady, even under the constant pressure he put on her. As she stood there with her head held high in defiance, something tugged at him.

God. Even her outspokenness is refreshing.

"What if it was yours?"

She shook her head. "What are you *talking* about?" she asked in exasperation before turning back to the bags to finish packing.

Lachlan crossed the room and blocked her path. "I realize I didn't always show my appreciation."

She snorted at that and pushed past him.

"But," he added while skirting in front of her again, "I want to find a way to fix that. It's my fault for being so absorbed in my work. I should have done more to recognize all you did for the company and me. What if I gave you more stock options? A raise? A bonus? Your own office? More paid time off?"

She pressed her lips in a tight line. "What makes you think you can buy me? And don't make me laugh about the paid time off. If you haven't noticed, I never had the chance to use my days to begin with. And if I did, you still managed to interrupt that." She poked a finger into his chest. "Look at you now. I don't even work for you, yet you're *still* here."

"I'll be better. I'll respect your time."

She took a step closer, standing toe-to-toe with him. Her eyes narrowed again. She did her best to size him up, despite being a whole head shorter than him. "You ever think that maybe I have other dreams than being the assistant of Lachlan Hart?" Her voice was a rough whisper, pushing his hormones into overdrive.

Would she sound like that if she whispered dirty things to him behind closed doors?

Get it together, Lachlan. You're here to convince her to work for you, not to get into her pants. Don't shit where you eat.

He swallowed. "Like what?" He tried to keep the conversation neutral, even though his thoughts were anything but.

Charlie gave a dry laugh. "Like you care? Do you realize that in the three years I've worked for you, you almost never asked me anything personal?"

"That isn't true." He was starting to panic. If this was the way to sway her decision, he was in deep shit.

She stepped away, and he instantly missed the heat of her body. She sat at the small table in the corner of the kitchen. "Yeah? Then where did I grow up? Where did I go to college?"

Fuck. "South Carolina? Somewhere South."

"Georgia."

"For college, you went Hofstra."

"NYU. Same as you. You'd think you'd remember something so relatable." She let out a breath and leaned on her elbows, planting her hands on the tabletop. "Why would I want to work for someone like you again? You don't even know me, and I've spent what feels like every waking minute with you for three years." Charlie pinned him to the spot with her green stare. "We might as well be strangers." The edge in her tone hinted at something else, something that surprised him.

Was that hurt? Regret? If so, he needed to find out why if he ever had a chance of winning her over.

Lachlan took a seat across from her, trying to soften his approach. "You think I'd fly across the Atlantic for just anyone?" He lifted his lips in a small smile he'd hoped came off as a sheepish peace offering. Maybe it would let her guard down a little. Instead, she pushed back in her chair and gawked at him like he had two heads.

"What *is* that?"

He stared at her, gauging her reaction. "What?"

"Are you...smiling? Is that...is that a smile? You don't smile."

"I smile," he argued.

"I've seen you smile all of one time. When Matteo came to the office with his wife and son after his accident."

Lachlan's gut clenched. Matteo and Lachlan had gone on a celebratory ski trip in Vermont after they got their first big round of funding nearly four years ago. It was supposed to be their day to revel in their success. The investor's infusion of cash showed them they were worth believing in. That they had a whole future ahead of them.

But a misstep on the slopes had Matteo careening off the side of the mountain, skiing at breakneck speed.

And break his neck he did, along with irreversible brain damage. He was nearly paralyzed the first year after his accident. Rehab to learn how to walk again had taken longer with his memory loss. Even after he could walk on his own again, he was never the same. The brain damage had taken on a form of dementia. Many days, Matteo had a hard time remembering things from his past. Sometimes it was something that had happened only moments before.

Lachlan had always felt guilty about that day. It was his idea to go skiing, even though he knew Matteo wasn't at the same level skill-wise. He should have told Matteo to take it easy. He shouldn't have agreed to let him go down the Black Diamond with him. Maybe if Lachlan had taken those precautions, Matteo's new wife and child wouldn't have had to deal with a husband and father who only lived a shell of a life.

Lachlan had taken it upon himself to make the business as much of a success as he could. He pushed hard these past four years, growing it so it was profitable and the funds could support Matteo's family and the medical care he'd need for the rest of his life.

It was only a fraction of what Lachlan owed his best friend.

"He had a good day," Lachlan said, lost in his thoughts.

"He did."

Lachlan looked up, capturing Charlie's gaze. "You said there was something else you wanted to do. What is it?"

She hesitated, likely debating whether it was worth sharing. She gave in. "I'm going to a UX bootcamp. I'm changing careers."

"UX?"

She glared at him defensively. "Yes, UX. I have other skills outside of managing your inbox."

He held up his hands in surrender. "I wasn't doubting you. It was just unexpected."

The ferry horn sounded in the distance. Charlie shot up from her chair, looking panicked. "Lachlan, what time is it?"

He checked his phone. "Just after five." Realization dawned on him. "*Fuck*."

She pointed to the grocery bags on the counter. "Throw those in the truck." She ran upstairs to get a backpack and locked the door behind them.

Hopping into the truck, she yelled for him to get in. She threw the truck into gear barely before he closed the door and barreled down the hill. She took a bend so sharply, Lachlan was convinced they were tilted on two wheels. She made it to the main road, speeding to the dock where the ferry waited.

Or would have waited. But it was too late.

They jumped out of the truck, leaving the doors ajar, as they raced down the wooden dock. Charlie screamed at the top of her lungs until her voice became hoarse.

The ferry had already left the dock, its shape getting smaller on the horizon.

Charlie ran a hand through her hair and paced. "Shit. Shit. Shit."

Lachlan stood there at a loss. If he thought winning her over before was tough, it was going to be damn near impossible now, especially with the venomous look in her eyes.

Throwing her hands at his chest, she pushed him, but his broad frame stayed steady as her delicate hands beat at him. He let her pummel him until she lost steam. "This is your fault, Lachlan. If you hadn't come here and distracted me, I would have made the ferry."

He grabbed her wrists gently, trying to calm her down. "I didn't intend to, Charlie. I'm sorry."

She ripped her wrists from his hands and put distance between them. "Because of you, we're stuck on this island. An island, need I remind you, that's in the path of a major storm. We're stranded!"

CHAPTER TEN

THIS CAN'T BE HAPPENING. We're sitting ducks, directly in the path of a storm. We won't make it. The crumbling cottage won't protect us if it's as bad as predicted.

Blood roared between Charlie's ears, making it impossible to concentrate. Damn Lachlan for showing up unexpectedly. If it weren't for him, she would have made it to the port in time. Now, there was no telling what they'd have to endure.

Charlie had grown up in an area prone to hurricanes. Even living in New York, she'd dealt with the disaster from Hurricane Sandy. Although the Isle of Murdina was used to rough winds in the winter, were the buildings sound enough to take on a storm system uncommon for the area?

She shook her head, trying to hear something other than the pounding of her frantic heartbeat. They couldn't be stranded here. There had to be some other way they could get off the island before it was too late.

Charlie raced to the truck and slid into the driver's seat. Again, Lachlan barely made it into the passenger side when she threw the truck in reverse, skidding on loose stone and sand, and shifted back to drive.

"Jesus, Charlie. Slow down!" Lachlan fumbled to put his seat belt on as she sped up the hill to the cottage.

She barreled around a turn and pulled to a rough stop in front of the cottage. Slamming her door shut, she bolted inside and to the kitchen.

"What are you doing?" Lachlan asked as he came into the room behind her, looking a little worse for the wear.

He unbuttoned the top button of his shirt and ran a hand through his thick dark hair. The shadows under his eyes were pronounced, not typical for him. The minor flaw almost made him seem more human.

"Looking for a radio," she responded from inside the walk-in pantry. She shoved a hand out of the pantry door and pointed to the back of the house. "There's a small shed off the back patio. See if you can find anything."

"Okay." He obliged without complaint and disappeared.

She used the brief reprieve to take a cleansing breath. She wasn't sure what rattled her more: Lachlan's unexpected appearance or the impending storm. Both felt equally dangerous.

Coming up empty-handed on the main floor, Charlie took the stairs two at a time. Her pulse spiked, and her skin felt sticky with sweat from the exertion and adrenaline. She pushed her loose hair behind her ears as she swung open the door to the hall's linen closet.

Empty.

She gave the upstairs a shakedown, checking every closet, under every bed, and in all the drawers of the sparsely furnished house. She rechecked the attic even though she knew nothing was up there from when she had inspected the roof with Kennedy.

She went back downstairs and pushed through the new back door, finding Lachlan exiting the storage shed.

"Anything?" she asked, a mix of fear and hope lacing her voice.

"No. Nothing useful."

"Shit." She bit her bottom lip.

"So now what?"

"I don't know. There has to be some other way to get in touch with someone from the mainland. Maybe the coast guard or someone can get us."

"You have cell service?" He untucked his shirt and rolled up his sleeves, showing off defined forearms with a smattering of dark hair.

A ping of interest shot through her. *Does the rest of his body have the same definition?* She shook her head, trying to rid herself of unwanted thoughts. "No. You?"

"No."

"We could break into the stores on the main road. Maybe they'll have something."

He took a step closer to her, making her pulse spike again, now for different reasons. Did his blue eyes always have a hint of green? The day-old stubble on his face made the outline of his jaw more pronounced. Sexy.

Are you insane? This is not the time. And definitely *not with him.*

"Charlie," he said as soothingly as he could, pulling her from the internal battle of poorly timed hormones, "those stores are closed up good and tight. We have nothing here that can help us get through those. No wire cutters. No crowbars. No ax. Nothing."

Charlie clenched and unclenched her fists. "This can't be it. We can't be out of options."

He rested two large hands on her shoulders and bent down to look her in the eyes. His gaze demanded to be seen. Temporarily hypnotized, she couldn't turn away. "I think we need to prepare to be stuck here."

She tried to shake his hands away, but he gripped lightly, holding her in place.

"We have to find another way off this island." Her argument was weak. Even if she wanted to stay in denial a little longer, deep down, she knew he was right.

"They aren't coming back for us. Not until the storm passes."

Her chest constricted, making it hard to breathe. She tried to suck in air as a panic attack threatened to suffocate her. "We're trapped," she finally said with acceptance.

"Hey." Lachlan took her chin between his thumb and forefinger, forcing her to focus on him again. Despite working in an office, Charlie felt the roughness of his fingers, something strangely unexpected. "We'll be okay."

"How can you know that? We barely have supplies, and the cottage is in rough shape."

"Rumor has it, I'm a pretty intelligent guy." He gave a small smile. Charlie glared at him. "And you're very capable. Between the two of us, we can figure out how to survive the storm as we wait it out." He stared out to the trees swaying in the wind and frowned. "Maybe it won't be as bad as we think." The inflection in his statement didn't do anything to ease her nerves.

Charlie pulled back from him. This time he allowed it. "Why couldn't you have left me alone?"

Her panic had turned into anger again. At least anger was safer than whatever unnecessary attraction she was having. It was Devonny's fault. She put it in Charlie's head that she'd now have time to date again. Her mind and body were just catching up with that idea. It wasn't because she *actually* thought there was a spark between them. Or maybe it was a side effect of stress. Wasn't there a proven theory that people felt things like lust and love toward another person when they're connected through a traumatic event?

That's all this was.

Right? *Right?*

"We wouldn't be in this situation if you just accepted that I quit," she continued, determined to create a pronounced line neither of them would dare to cross. She almost laughed at the thought of Lachlan wanting to cross a line with someone like her. "If you would have let me go, this would be different."

"I can't change the fact that I came here to try to win you back." His voice was low and serious. The words hung between them as they stared at each other.

That was the most vulnerable thing I've ever heard him say. He came here for me. She paused at that, her heart thumping wildly against her chest.

Her ego was playing tricks on her. He hadn't come here for *her*—he had come because he needed his assistant. That realization was enough to raise her defenses again.

"And now our lives might be in danger because you're too damn stubborn." She exhaled a shaky breath. "Just leave me alone, Lachlan."

He looked up to the sky and let out a harsh laugh. He fixed his gaze on her, this time with heat and anger behind it. "Leave you alone? We're the only two people left on this godforsaken island. You can't honestly think this is my fault."

She threw up her hands. "Of course it is! You were never supposed to be here. I was *supposed* to be able to move on with my life. To forge a new future. Now, I'm not even sure I'll have one if the storm wipes us off the planet."

"I'll do everything I can to keep us safe."

"Do whatever the hell you want. Just stay away from me."

Charlie stormed into the house, her emotions frayed. Seeing him here in this unusual situation was confusing. She was so angry at him. Frustrated. But the way he looked at her and the gentle way he touched her face stirred something in the deepest parts of her. His voice—gravelly and deep, promising to keep her safe—twisted her stomach in knots.

Asking him to leave her be was self-preservation. Something about his rough honesty had her wanting to find out more about the man she'd tried her hardest to distance herself from. Lachlan Hart had no business being here, and she sure as hell had no business wondering what was beyond his cool, distant exterior.

* * *

Charlie had hidden away in the master bedroom, pacing for nearly an hour, as she tried to work through the conflicting feelings coursing through her. She was scared of this unpredictable storm. Worried the house wouldn't withstand the onslaught of rain and wind. Unsettled over the fact that Lachlan was under the same roof as her. Panicked knowing he was so close in proximity to her, but for the life of her, she couldn't understand why that had her insides churning.

A tentative knock on the bedroom door interrupted her thoughts.

"What?" she grounded out testily.

"Can I come in? Please?" He sounded strained on the last word.

She snorted. Must be hard for a man like Lachlan to ask for anything.

"Fine."

He slowly opened the creaky door, peeking in as if to see if it was safe. "I brought you something to eat." He came in with a small tray filled with sliced cheese, meat, and bread. "I hope it's okay. I saw this when I took the bags from the truck."

She sighed. "We should really consider rationing the food. We don't know how long we'll be stuck here."

He nodded. "I already sorted that out. I gathered what you had left and wrote notes on how much we could eat each day. We will be okay with this even if we're stuck here for nearly a week. I also pulled in as much firewood as I could from the shed."

Charlie was thankful she'd bought more food than needed when she went to the store. She had no idea how they would have survived if she hadn't. "Thank you."

"I found jugs in the pantry and filled them with water. We have about eight gallons' worth."

"That was smart." She eyed him.

He shrugged. "I was in the Boy Scouts. I remember a few things from our camping trips. Also, we should eat the perishable foods first since they won't last if or when the electricity goes out."

He passed her a plate as she took a seat on the edge of the bed. When he didn't make a motion to move, she rolled her eyes and reluctantly patted a spot next to her. He sat.

She felt awkward with him sitting next to her. They always had something between them, whether it was a desk, conference table, or one of her to-do lists. But now, the heat of his body warmed her arm and thigh, and she kind of liked it. She wanted to scold her body for betraying her, even over something so trivial.

She wasn't sure if the reaction was caused by his presence or the fact that he was trying to be a decent human. Either way, she didn't want to look too deeply into it. The sooner she could put distance between them, the better.

She took a bite of the day-old, crusty bread and eyed the tumblers of amber liquid on the tray. "What's that?"

He lifted a glass and handed it to her. "Scotch. I picked it up on my way here. I figured we could have discussed your reemployment over a glass."

Charlie picked up the tumbler and inspected it. "I don't like Scotch." She tossed her head back and downed the drink in one gulp, the heat of it burning the whole way down. She sputtered out a cough.

"Whoa. You're supposed to sip it."

She shrugged one shoulder. "Desperate times, and all of that." She grabbed his glass and took another heaping gulp, finishing it off quickly. She needed something to take the edge off.

Lachlan stared at her, his dark eyebrows raised. "That was a nice bottle of Scotch. Meant to be savored."

Charlie's lips twitched into an almost smile. "I think you can afford it."

He let out a long breath. "Listen, I get it. You're pissed at me. And although I don't agree with your anger, I'll say I'm sorry if it means we can be amicable."

Charlie snapped her head in his direction. "You're a really shitty apologizer."

"I don't feel like I should apologize." He took a bite of his cheese casually.

"Island mishap aside, you were a terrible boss."

He faced her, fury making his deep-blue eyes flash to a shade of green, angry like the ocean water pounding the island below. "Excuse me?"

"I said you were a shitty boss." She emphasized every word, hoping it would cause him to storm out and give her the space she needed. Each second with him caused a flurry of confused emotions, ones she didn't have the energy to deal with.

The Lachlan Hart on this island wasn't the same Lachlan Hart from New York. There, he was cold, calculated, and distant. Here, he was trying, helpful, and dare she say, chatty.

"You realize this is the longest non-work-related conversation you and I have ever had, right?" He turned away and looked straight ahead to the wall across the room. Shaking his head lightly, he sighed. "I'm sorry."

She wasn't expecting that response, and not in the honest way he said it. She opened and closed her mouth, not sure how to reply.

"I'm very serious about my work," Lachlan continued. "Matteo and I had a dream to build the company together. Without him, it's a lot to take on. A lot's at stake. Many people—Matteo, his family, and every single employee—need this to work. We did well the first few years, but competition is gaining on us."

Charlie's defenses wavered under his explanation. For years, she thought Lachlan was just obsessed with creating the best of the best in AI and machine learning. That everything he did was about ego and status. She thought he wanted to be the next Tesla or Apple or Microsoft.

Now, she was seeing that being the best wasn't for himself; it was for those who helped make the company what it was. It was for Matteo and every employee who still rallied behind the mission with unwavering passion.

She sneaked a glance at him, inspecting the hard edges of seriousness on his face. How his dark eyebrows lowered over piercing eyes, the contrast making them more vibrant. How his full lips were pressed tightly together in deep concentration, as if the weight of the world was becoming all too much to bear. He lifted a large hand to rub the day-old dark stubble on his defined chin.

Oh no.

Sure, she had always thought Lachlan Hart was attractive, but his personality and standoffishness had made it easy to not blur the lines like many other women had tried to do.

And now? Understanding a bit more about his drive?

She was in trouble.

CHAPTER ELEVEN

LACHLAN FELT some of Charlie's chilly exterior melt away when he'd met her in her bedroom earlier, but it was short-lived. Something shifted during their chat. As much as he kept people at arm's length, he was fairly inept in sensing their body language. He had a way of figuring out what they wanted to say even if they didn't come right out with it.

And the way Charlie's body suddenly went ramrod straight and how she shifted ever so slightly—attempting and failing at doing it discreetly—so they weren't touching said it all.

She still didn't trust him. That was a hurdle he had to get over if he was going to convince her to come back.

And he *was* going to convince her.

Maybe getting stuck on the island would give him more time to chip away at her strong will and get her to see why working for him made sense. At least now he had a small idea of what she was interested in. He knew all the facilitators at the best bootcamps in New York and San Francisco. Surely he could work out a deal with them. Maybe a special one-on-one course in UX that would allow her to learn while also working for him. It would be a win-win.

He mulled over what would happen after she completed the bootcamp. She wouldn't want to stay as his assistant, which wasn't ideal. That meant she would still leave him eventually. But if he could set up the work-and-learn deal with one of the bootcamps, he could get another year out of her. She'd still be there to support him through some of the biggest moments for the company.

And if he had a year before she went, he'd be able to seek out another solid assistant, one Charlie could train so there would be a seamless transition.

Without her. He swallowed hard.

Why did that feel so wrong?

Sensing Charlie's need to be alone, Lachlan busied himself downstairs, finding opportunities to secure the house before the storm came. He swung open the loose cabinet doors under the kitchen sink and slid in to inspect the piping, remembering it acting up earlier when he was filling jugs with water. Pulling a wrench from a rusty old toolbox he found in the storage shed, he got to work.

Manual labor had always helped Lachlan think. Naturally curious, he had loved tinkering with things while growing up. As a kid, his mother would get furious when she'd find his new toys completely pulled apart. But anger soon turned into fascination when she watched him put them back together without an instruction manual in sight.

By his early teenage years, he had become obsessed with understanding how things worked. How they were put together. Why certain combinations caused things to function in a specific way, but one small tweak could create a completely different outcome. By his senior year in high school, he had built his first computer from scratch.

Yet as much as he knew about how many things worked, he couldn't fight the doubt that there was one thing he wouldn't be able to figure out: how to get Charlie back.

Seeing her here made his body hum with awareness. Something

about the way she pushed back and said what was on her mind was intoxicating. For years, people had walked on eggshells around him— even her—always trying to portray the best versions of themselves.

Being a multimillionaire tech genius would do that.

He wasn't sure when it started; he just remembered noticing it one day. People treated him differently. They took their time speaking to him in a polished way. He could see their nervousness or hunger, trying to put their best foot forward. Wanting to impress him. Angling to be part of his "inner circle" as if it were some magical place where all their hopeful dreams could come true.

But these "perfect" versions of people made him feel alienated. He never knew who he was really dealing with, and he missed the easy way people would talk and collaborate openly. Lachlan often wondered if they only tried to get in his good graces to use his status to propel their careers and personal lives forward.

As the years went on, he found himself wishing he was back in his shitty Hoboken apartment with Matteo, developing the best algorithm, the one who made them who they were today. Those were the days. They would shoot the shit, working side by side on their code. They'd eat day-old pizza, drink cheap beer, laugh a little too loudly, and curse when things didn't go well. They were just...normal.

Being here with Charlie made him feel normal again. Although she was never the type to put on a front as the others had, she'd often been too focused on doing a good job to show this side of herself. She wanted to get the work done, and she wanted to get it done right. And with how much work he threw at her, there wasn't much time for her to be anything but the efficient employee he could count on.

But today? She had his blood pumping and made him feel like he was coming out of a fog. He felt alive.

"What are you doing?" Her voice startled him, causing him to jump up and slam his head.

"Fuck!" Sliding out from under the sink, he rubbed the sore spot with a free hand.

Charlie rushed to his side and kneeled, putting her soft hand to his head. "I'm sorry. I didn't mean to surprise you."

He propped up on his elbow, making no motion to move. He loved the feel of her fingers on his skin and wanted nothing more than to let the moment linger a little longer. When was the last time a woman's touch made him feel...anything? "It's just a bump. I'll survive."

They paused, and their eyes locked. Her fingertips slid delicately across his face as if they had a mind of their own, stroking his cheek and pushing back his hair. Shock crossed her features, and she dropped her hand to her lap. He wanted to reach out and grab it again.

Don't stop touching me ever.

"Sounded louder than a bump." She inspected his face with reluctance, her large green eyes focusing where it stung, not daring to meet his gaze again. "I don't think we have ice here."

He shook his head and pushed to stand up. She stood too. "I'm okay. I didn't hit it too hard. It might not even bruise."

"You sure?"

He grinned and pointed to the sink with the wrench. "Yeah. I was going to fix this sink and then get dinner started."

She tilted her head and wrinkled her nose. "Dinner?"

Leaning a hip against the counter, he smiled again. "Yeah. Might surprise you, but I can do more than cut bread and cheese."

She bit her plush bottom lip, and he ached to find out what her mouth felt like. "You don't have to cook dinner—"

"I insist. We had a rocky start today. Consider it a gesture of goodwill."

He kneeled back down to work on the sink while Charlie shuffled across the small kitchen to the pantry where Lachlan had placed the grocery bags. From under the cabinet, he could hear her looking through the groceries he'd arranged based on how perishable it was and their ration sizes. A plastic bag crinkled, followed by footsteps. The refrigerator door opened and closed.

"What can you do with lettuce?" she finally asked.

"With the leftover cold cuts and cheese, I could make a salad. Might be a little dry without any dressing."

"It is what it is," she said, dejection in her voice.

Lachlan made a few tweaks to the pipe and put it back together. Sliding out from under the cabinet, he turned on the faucet. The water flowed smoothly down the drain. "Looks good."

"Good job." Her voice was flat. She eyed him up and down. "Did you bring any other clothes? I mean, who flies overnight and works on plumbing in a button-down and slacks?"

"Yeah. I grabbed my overnight bag from my last trip."

Charlie nodded. "Assuming you didn't remove anything, you have a few casual pieces in there."

Lachlan shoved a hand through his thick hair, completely forgetting Charlie had taken it upon herself to organize everything in his life, including packing for his trips. "I had the hotel send out for laundry before I flew back, so I didn't bother unpacking when I returned. Everything's there."

Regarding him warily, she spun on her heel and marched to the pantry. He cursed under his breath, sensing her walls coming back up again. Making progress with her was going to be harder than he thought.

She returned with a half-opened bottle of red wine. Pouring herself a glass, she held it up in an offering. Her reservations were still evident in her eyes despite the gesture.

He shook his head. "I'll get myself some Scotch."

She raised her eyebrows and made a face. "Of course, how could I forget?" she said, her dry sarcasm almost too forced, and took a sip of wine. "What were you planning on accomplishing with that anyway? Think you could get me buzzed so you could throw me over your shoulder caveman-style and drag me back to New York?"

His lips quirked as he tried to hide a smile. "Had there been transportation back from the island, that might have been the better option."

And if I were to throw you over my shoulder, it'd be on the way to my bed. He coughed and shook his head, trying to release whatever horny hold she had over him.

Charlie ran a hand down her face. "Look, Lachlan." Her serious tone pulled him from his internal battle of wills. "Whatever you say or do won't be enough to convince me to change my mind. I've made a decision, and I'm going to see it through." She lifted the wineglass and paused halfway to her lips. "I owe it to myself," she said more to herself than to him.

We'll see about that.

Before he could press more, they both were startled by the loud rattling from the wood planks covering the windows. Charlie put down her glass and rushed upstairs to her bedroom. Lachlan followed close behind.

They looked out the window. The clouds had become thick and dark, swallowing the last bit of dusk light they could see. Below, empty plastic flowerpots and trash cans rolled along the street. Newly planted trees bent severely, the wind threatening to break the tiny trunks like twigs.

Inside the house, Lachlan could only hear Charlie's harsh, fast breathing. He put a hand on her shoulder, gently encouraging her to turn toward him. Her large eyes almost looked comical, now even wider from worry.

"We'll be okay. I promise." He pushed a strand of red hair behind her ear, a gesture meant to soothe her, but the feel of her sent a surge of lust through him.

If he dipped his head a few inches lower, he could capture those lips that had tempted him all day.

So close...

She looked up at him, her voice holding the slightest quiver. "How do you know that? The storm isn't even here yet, and the wind is already picking up."

The roof groaned under the next gust of wind. Their heads tilted up, half expecting the roof to be ripped off. Charlie shot him a frightened look, and Lachlan instinctively pulled her into his arms. Every fiber of his being wanted to keep her safe.

At the next large creak, Lachlan wondered if he'd be able to keep his promise.

CHAPTER TWELVE

THERE WAS a break in the wind later that evening, and the unsettling groan from the roof eventually subsided. Without the loud noises, the tension had eased enough so Charlie could stomach eating dinner. All through their meal—which was dry, but was somehow still delicious thanks to the herbs Lachlan had "borrowed" from the neighbor's garden—he had managed to take her mind off the impending doom outside.

The conversation was light and noninvasive, and whenever a violent burst of wind startled her, he found a way to make her laugh. There were times she could have sworn she saw a look of hunger in his eyes.

And not for the food.

She had watched him lick his full, kissable lips whenever his gaze had fallen on her mouth. But as soon as their eyes locked, the hooded look was gone.

Charlie retreated to bed after dinner, exhausted from the stress of the day and needing space from Lachlan. Her mind was a jumbled mess seeing him here. He was the enemy, yet...

She tried to snap herself out of it. First Kennedy and now him?

She was convinced the attraction was all in her head, likely the result of going a little *too* long without male companionship.

But when Lachlan had wrapped her in his arms earlier, she couldn't deny all the conflicting emotions firing off: lust, excitement, anxiety, shame.

However, out of all the feelings, curiosity was the winner.

What would a guy like Lachlan Hart want with someone like her? Someone so *normal?*

She'd seen the types of women who had attended high-profile events with him. Hell, she helped organize it half of the time. Charlie had also seen the kinds of women who threw themselves at him, which he gracefully dodged. If they couldn't capture his attention, why would she? A simple Southern girl who only recently found some direction to her life.

More importantly, why did it matter?

Lachlan wasn't Charlie's type anyway. She preferred men who were down-to-earth, kind, open, and not so serious. Someone like Kennedy.

Basically, all the things Lachlan wasn't.

But when she caught his gaze fixated on her mouth on more than one occasion, she couldn't stop her stomach from doing a little flip. Somehow, that one look—whether it was real or a figment of her imagination—had made her feel desired in ways she never had been before.

She almost hoped he would press her about coming back to MindThrive AI. At least then she could remember why she needed to keep her barriers up and why the last three years of her life had been unfulfilled thanks to his constant needs cutting into her personal time.

But he never brought it up. Instead, he focused on keeping her calm and easing her obvious worry.

Still, she waited, knowing he wasn't one to give up so easily. She was sure he'd pounce as soon as she let her guard down even the slightest bit. She'd seen him in boardrooms, client pitches, and negotiations. Lachlan was a man who got what he wanted. He commanded a room and dominated a conversation with few words. He wasn't a talker, but when he did, his words made an impact.

Which was why it was so unnerving to share a casual meal with him tonight. He was almost...charming.

At some point that night, Charlie fell into a fitful sleep. Dreams about Lachlan's deep-blue eyes looking down at her while he hovered over her—both of them naked—had her tossing and turning. Her dreams were so lucid, so real. She could almost feel the weight of his body on her, the feel of his smooth skin as she ran her hand along his back.

The way he filled her up so perfectly.

A loud shatter startled her awake. She found herself showered in glass and jumped from the bed. As she reached for the bedside lamp, sharp pain shot up her foot. The wind blew fiercely, the tree outside smacking against the house and into the now-broken bedroom window.

Bare footsteps on the wooden floor sounded from the hallway, getting louder by the second. Lachlan threw open her bedroom door, his dark hair disheveled, his face full of concern.

He was naked from the waist up, making her forget all about the throbbing pain in her foot.

Now, the throbbing migrated someplace else, and it most definitely didn't feel painful.

Charlie's heart lurched in her throat. How was it he managed to look *better* than in her racy dreams? His broad shoulders led down to rounded pectorals. His stomach was flat with the ridges of a six-pack. His lats were wide, as if she could use them to hold on to while he gave her the ride of her life. Narrow hips disappeared into his sweat pants, which hid the one thing she was truly curious about.

Her face heated and warmth pooled between her legs in an instant.

How did he hide all of *that* under those suits and she'd never noticed? Surely she would have seen the strain of his back muscles if he moved or the bulge of his biceps when he picked something up?

She shifted, instinctively taking a step toward him, desperate to reach out and feel all the wonders he'd hidden from her. Pain shot through her foot again, and she cried out, falling onto the bed. Another sharp pain cut through her hand.

"Stay right there." His voice was commanding. Sexy.

The urge to touch him again consumed her, briefly distracting her from the pain. Thankfully, he raced out of the room before she could act on it, appearing a moment later wearing running shoes.

Charlie squeaked when he crossed the room in two steps and unexpectedly scooped her in his arms like he was a superhero saving her from a burning building. She pressed her face against the crook of his neck and inhaled his scent: a mix of wood, smoke, and a bit of salty sweat.

The scruff on his jaw scraped against her cheek, and in a daze, she reached up to touch it. She ran her fingertips along his sandpaper-rough jawline and traced his bottom lip. Soft yet firm.

His Adam's apple bobbed as his lips parted, examining her from the corner of his eye. For a moment, his steps faltered as if torn between taking care of her and just taking her right there.

It's all in your head, Charlie.

Her well-being must have taken priority. Lachlan picked up the pace again, pushing open the bathroom door with his foot, and closed the lid of the toilet before placing her gently on it.

"First-aid kit?" He turned to the medicine cabinet and opened it, finding nothing.

"I'm not sure. There wasn't much here when I arrived." She looked at her hand. A small shard of glass peeking out from an open wound glinted in the light. Charlie, never good with blood, grew dizzy.

Lachlan frowned. "Jesus. You're as white as a ghost. Head between your knees." His voice was rough and determined.

I want your *head between my knees.* A giggle escaped her lips as delirium set in.

"Charlie," he said, pulling her from her fuzzy thoughts. "Head. Between. Your. Knees."

She nodded seriously, trying to hide the fact that she felt drunk from her heightened blood pressure, and did as she was told.

Crouched down, he opened the cabinet under the sink and stuck a hand toward the deep, dark crevices in the back. Cursing under his breath, he raced out of the bathroom and down the stairs, coming back with kitchen scissors and one of the new white towels she'd bought before coming here.

He turned on the faucet for the claw-foot tub, testing the water to ensure it was warm without scalding. "You think you can walk over here to clean out your cuts?"

Charlie raised her head, still feeling woozy. She nodded slowly.

Lachlan held out a hand, engulfing hers as he helped her to her good foot. He guided her to the tub, a look of deep concentration on his face. She dipped her injured foot into the stream of water and winced. "I think the glass is still in there."

Sitting her back on the toilet, Lachlan kneeled before her, gently taking her foot and raising it. He made a face. "You have any tweezers?"

"In my makeup bag." She pointed a limp finger to a small canvas bag sitting near the sink.

He went through the bag, treating it as if it might detonate if he touched the wrong thing. Pulling out a pair of pointy tweezers, he scrubbed them with soap and water before kneeling again.

"This might hurt," he warned as he lifted her foot. "I'll try to fish it out as quickly as possible, but it's pretty deep."

"O-Okay." Charlie bit her lower lip as he moved the tweezers to her foot. She flinched right before he touched her.

He looked up from under his dark eyebrows, his face serious. "You have to stay still. Otherwise, I'll end up hurting you more."

She let out a breath. "I'm sorry."

He looked back to her foot, bringing the tweezers to the glass. She could feel pressure and a sharp pain as he got a hold of the glass. The tweezers slipped as he tried to dislodge it. A whimper escaped her.

"I'm sorry," he whispered as he went back in to retrieve it again, this time with success. She held out her hand for him to inspect. "I think one splintered off in there."

Charlie gave him a worried look. "What's that mean?"

"Means I'll have to dig in there a couple of times to get it all out."

"Lach," she said in a small voice. "I'm very squeamish."

Charlie sucked in a breath as he placed a warm, tender kiss on the inside of her wrist. The feel of his soft lips on her sensitive skin made her light-headed all over again.

A flash of surprise crossed his face, and he suddenly focused harder on her hand, not meeting her eyes. "I'll try to make it quick."

She watched him move with precision, trying to distract herself from the pressure of the tweezers digging into her wound. Her gaze roved over his body, taking in his smooth skin and rounded shoulders that led to something unexpected.

"What's that?" she asked, her voice shaky from nausea.

He smiled to himself, a sexy, mysterious one that had her already twisted stomach twisting more. "I take it you mean my tattoo."

With her uninjured hand, Charlie traced the large tattoo covering his shoulder and part of his chest. A shiver ran through her when she outlined the artwork on the sinewy muscles of his upper body. The colors were a mix of dark blues, greens, and grays. The artwork was masterful, full of calming swirls and a bit of danger. "I never would have taken you for someone with ink."

"I got it in my early twenties. It represented who I was at the time. A beach bum who was passionate about surfing."

She looked at him in disbelief. "You? A surfer? But you're so..."

His eyes twinkled playfully in the bathroom light. "Serious? Uptight? What else was it that you called me?"

"Distant. Cold."

"Of course. How could I forget?" he said dryly. "I grew up in a small beach town, and I lived for the days of good surf. My mother would have a fit when I went out there, even in the dead of winter or when swells came in from a big storm, but I loved it. It helped me unwind, something that was hard to do when my brain was so focused on tech."

Charlie swallowed a lump in her throat as he talked about his favorite surfing memories, the stories distracting her from the pain. She learned how his father had taught him and his older brother when they were young kids. First, starting with boogie boards.

"My dad gave me my first surfboard when I was nine. It was one of his growing up. Aside from a few dings he patched up, it was in great shape. My dad, brother, and I would surf all day, only taking a break to grab sandwiches and soda Mom had waiting for us on the beach." His voice was deep and quiet as if he were lost in those memories.

"It sounds nice." Her comment seemed to bring him back from whatever memory he'd lost himself in. She almost didn't want to interrupt. She loved learning more about this other side of him and didn't want to ruin the moment.

He sighed. "It was a different time."

"Do you do it anymore? Surf?"

"No." He frowned. As he shared his story, she could somehow imagine it clearly. Those broad shoulders paddling through the waves. His lean hips expertly twisting with the barrels. Maybe he was no longer a surfer, but the physique stayed the same.

And it was a damn good physique.

He held her hand steady, pulling out two small pieces from the wound. She flinched. "Are you almost done?" she asked, her stomach turning again.

He pulled out one last shard. "All done."

She looked down to the bleeding cut. "Will I need stitches?"

He shook his head, his dark hair falling slightly over his forehead.

"I'm no doctor, but neither looked deep enough to warrant for it. Let's get them cleaned out and wrapped up."

She cringed. "Not my new towels."

His lips twitched. "Tell you what. I promise to buy you a new set once we make it off this island. Deal?"

The lights of the vanity became blinding. "I guess." Charlie's head felt fuzzy again, making her nearly faint. She straightened, took a shaky breath, and swallowed hard. She was vulnerable under Lachlan's care, but something deep in her gut made her want to trust him. Not because he was the only person on this damn island who could help her, but because she could sense that he actually cared.

Or maybe you're just delusional from nearly fainting.

He helped her to the tub again, washing out her wounds with gentle hands. He took the scissors and split the towel up in strips, wrapping up her foot and hand securely.

Exhaustion washed over Charlie.

"You okay?" he asked, as her eyes started to drift closed.

"Adrenaline is wearing off." She barely had the energy to reply.

Lachlan pulled her into his arms again and lifted her up, cradling her against his bare torso. She snuggled her head against him, mindlessly trailing her finger along the planes of his chest and through the light smattering of dark hair, not caring about the lines she was crossing.

"Where are you going?" she asked quietly as he passed her room.

"I'm not letting you sleep in a bed full of broken glass."

"Oh."

He pushed open the door to his room with a knee and rested her on the bed. Pulling a blanket over her, he tucked her in. "Good?"

She nodded, snuggled in more, and closed her eyes.

Lachlan crossed the room, the sound of rustling coming from the floor.

"Lach?" she whispered, her energy waning.

"Yeah."

"Where are you?"

"On the floor."

"Why?"

"I may be a red-blooded man, but I'd like to think I'm gentleman enough to allow a woman to have the bed when she's in a vulnerable state."

"You gonna bite if we share a bed?"

"If I'm lucky," it sounded like he mumbled.

"What?"

"Nothing, Charlie. Go to sleep. You had a rough night."

She squiggled down in the bed to get more comfortable. Turning on her side, she inhaled Lachlan's scent lingering on the pillows. She smiled.

"Lach?"

"Yes, Charlie," he said on a sigh.

"Thank you."

And with that, she fell asleep, once again dreaming about the man sleeping only mere feet from her.

CHAPTER THIRTEEN

LACHLAN WOKE to a warm body stirring against him and the soft noises of someone in a deep sleep. He opened a heavy eyelid.

Where the hell am I?

A stream of dull white light flowed through a small window and landed on the bed, illuminating Charlie's red hair and making the copper highlights shine like spun gold.

Then he remembered.

At some point, in a half-asleep state, Charlie's sweet Southern voice had called out, coaxing him to come to bed. Although the daytime had been balmy sixty-something degrees, the temperature had dropped throughout the night. Without heating or air conditioning, the stone cottage, with all its broken windows, had become frigid.

The sound of her sleepy voice cutting through the quiet room had made his insides churn and his manhood twitch. It was like a siren's song pulling him deeper into dangerous territory, but so alluring, he didn't care. She made him reckless. Keeping things professional was the furthest thing from his mind when he heard her soft murmurs. His name falling from her lips was a new addiction.

An addiction he needed to kick.

Lachlan wasn't the kind of guy to go for his assistants. In fact, he had a rule about not fraternizing with *anyone* he worked with. But damn her for making him question the strength of his willpower.

Climbing into bed with Charlie and all her soft, luscious curves—curves he only discovered yesterday—was trouble. It was bad enough he didn't have the sense to *not* give in to her, but on more than one occasion, he had to fight the urge to reach out to her, take her in his arms, and crash his lips onto hers.

She shifted again. In the night, Lachlan must have wrapped an arm around her when Charlie had nestled against him. Her body molded to his, fitting every nook and cranny.

Especially the way her ass pressed perfectly against his crotch.

The realization had him hard in an instant.

Fuck.

Trying not to disturb Charlie and call attention to his *situation,* he reluctantly pulled away from her. He needed some space. Maybe a cold shower. Something to keep whatever unusual feelings he was having for his assistant at bay.

After throwing on an undershirt, he padded downstairs quietly. Checking his phone, he found it was barely dawn, despite there not being nearly any sunlight to show for it. The dark clouds and relentless rain were ominous and oppressive. The house occasionally groaned, worrying Lachlan that the malicious storm would break through their only means of survival.

He looked at his cell again, half hoping by some miracle he'd find a nondead spot for service. After walking around the main floor while holding his phone in varying degrees, he realized it was pointless. Not only would he miss the meeting with the investors today, but he had no way of telling anyone he wasn't going to make it.

Devonny knew he had flown to Scotland to go after Charlie. Maybe she'd give people a heads-up when he'd appeared to be MIA.

He ran a hand down his face and let out a breath. He hoped his "flaking out" wouldn't kill the deal with the VC firm.

Hell, he hoped word didn't get out he ditched a meeting with investors in general. The VC community was small, and this could fuck him over with more investors than just this one.

"Lach?"

He swallowed and turned to find Charlie standing on the stairs, wrapped in the fluffy comforter, her hair a tousled mess. He loved the way she said his nickname, one he hadn't heard since he and Matteo had created the algorithm that essentially started MindThrive AI.

Since that day, everything had changed.

But hearing her say his name turned back time to when things were simpler. To when he was just *him* and not the tech superstar everyone was watching. The way it sounded, rolling softly off her tongue, felt intimate. Comfortable. Two things he hadn't had with a woman in years.

Casual sex, yes. But anything beyond that, not so much.

He wanted to pause this moment and stay there.

"I didn't mean to wake you." His murmur was rough from sleep.

She took the last steps down to meet him in the living room, limping slightly. "You didn't. The rain pounding on the window did."

He took her hand, trying to ignore the electricity crackling between them, and peeked under the makeshift wrappings. "How are you feeling?"

"A little sore. My hand doesn't feel as bad as my foot, but it's manageable." She looked up at him, her eyes sparkling in the dim light from the fire Lachlan had started. "I was a little out of it last night. If I haven't said it already, thank you." She stared at him for a moment longer, searching his face for what, he wasn't sure. But just as he thought she might lean in closer, she took a step back and turned away.

"You did thank me last night," he rushed to say, trying to stop her from retreating. He wanted those gorgeous eyes on him again. Needed to be *seen* by *her*. "But it's no problem. I'll get that window boarded up in a minute."

She shrugged. "Almost pointless now. Looks like a monsoon hit that room. All the rain blew in through the window. It's soaked, and there are leaves and branches everywhere. It's almost a wonder we slept at all last night with how this storm has picked up."

"I'm sorry. I should have thought to do it last night."

"It's okay. It just means…"

His breath lodged in his throat. "We're roommates for a little longer," he finished for her.

She nodded and looked down at her feet. "You don't need to sleep on the floor."

"Okay. Thanks." He tried to keep his voice steady despite the hammering of his heart.

"Have you seen what's going on outside?" She sounded less sheepish now that she was on a safe subject.

"I haven't had a chance." He held up his cell phone.

Charlie cringed. "No service still?" Lachlan shook his head. "Anyone know you're here?"

"Aside from Devonny, nope. Thought I'd be in and out."

Charlie wrapped herself tighter in the comforter, looking guilty. "I'm sorry. I know today was the investor meeting."

He shoved a hand through his hair and blew out a breath. "Let's just hope they're understanding."

Charlie jumped at the wind whistling through the boarded-up windows and the sound of bushes and trees banging against the house.

Right into his arms.

Lachlan held her tightly, savoring the feel of her warmth against his body. *Why does this feel so right?*

She pulled away enough to lock gazes with him, her lips parted. Time stood still as they stayed fused together, their faces only centimeters away.

Did she just lean in?

The urge to kiss her was all-consuming. She was there for the taking.

Don't you fucking dare.

Another loud thwack against the windows had her jumping back out of his arms. His stomach sank over the missed opportunity.

"It's still kinda dark, but maybe we can see what's going on outside the bedroom window." She didn't hesitate as she rushed toward the stairs, even with her bum foot, likely desperate to get away from him.

Lachlan followed and placed an arm around her, allowing her to use him as a crutch. He tried to ignore the buzzing in his body as her full hips bumped against him every other step.

What would it feel like to grab those hips while she was riding him?

Jesus Christ.

They made it to the bedroom just in time to give Lachlan the excuse to let her go. How the hell was he supposed to sleep next to her and battle his suddenly insatiable desire for her? Even in the morning hours, with her hair in a tangled mess and her eyes puffy from lack of sleep, he thought she was the most stunning woman he'd ever seen.

"Take a look at this," she said from the window, barely audible over the blood rushing through his ears.

Lachlan took a tentative step to the window, nervous that being any closer to her would be his willpower's undoing. He held his breath, trying to avoid inhaling that fading flowery-peppery scent of hers.

Peering through the heavy rain, he could see the bushes and trees thrashing around. Limbs had fallen to the ground or lay upon the roofs of the neighboring houses. In the distance, he looked out to the coast where the main road was. Squinting, he tried to make out what he was seeing.

"Where's the dock?"

Charlie nudged him aside so she could get a better look. She pressed her hands to the window and put her face in between them like she was creating makeshift binoculars. "I don't see it." She exhaled, her warm breath fogging a spot on the window.

"I can't tell if it's gone or if it's underwater. It looks like there's storm surge already."

"You don't think the surge will get that high, do you?" Her voice shook and eyes went wide.

"Depends on wind, currents, and high tide. I don't doubt it will flood the main road."

"And us? It couldn't get to us, right? In all the years I've dealt with hurricanes, I've never seen it creep up this high."

"We're on a hill—albeit a small one—but we're toward the bottom of the hill. I'd say we're maybe twenty or so feet above sea level." He made a face.

"What?" She wrapped the comforter tighter around her body.

"I think Hurricane Katrina produced something like twenty-five feet of storm surge."

"But that was a freak storm."

He pointed to the window. "And this isn't?"

Her shoulders sagged. "They said it was supposed to be unlike anything the island has ever seen. I thought maybe they were being overly sensational. You know, like the weather stations do sometimes for ratings."

"Let's hope." They froze in place as the lights flickered on and off. "You said there was a generator?"

She nodded. "Out back."

"I'll be right back," he said as he made his way downstairs.

She hobbled behind him. "You can't go out there! It's dangerous."

He threw her a pointed look over his shoulder that stopped her in her tracks. "Do you like electricity? Water?"

"Yes."

"Then let me get this sorted out. Did you and the property manager, Kevin or whatever—"

"Kennedy."

"Did he check it?"

"Not sure."

Lachlan slipped on his sneakers sitting by the back door. "You wouldn't have happened to have brought a jacket? Umbrella?"

Charlie's snort traveled down the stairs. Realizing he would have to deal with the onslaught of rain head on, he swung the door open and walked outside. He hoped he wouldn't get struck by lightning or electrocuted in the process.

Lachlan located the generator off to the side of the house, hidden by a few scraggly bushes. The wind gusts took him unexpectedly, knocking him to his knees and into a muddy puddle. Straightening, he wiped the raindrops from his eyes—as useless as that was—and trudged along the wet ground that sucked at his feet like quicksand.

Thunder rumbled, and a limb snapped from a neighbor's tree, falling to the ground with a wet thud. Lachlan kneeled near the generator, a flashlight in hand. Despite it being morning, the thick clouds made it hard to see. Flashing a stream of light on the machine, he noted its rough shape. It was ancient and rusted.

He stood and fought against the wind to get to the storage shed to see if there were any fuel or oil cans. Luckily, he found fuel storage tanks in the back corner and a canister of oil on a shelf. It wasn't much, but he hoped it would last at least a day or two if the going got tough. He already knew the small generator would only power a room or two at a time as it was.

Despite the poor conditions, Lachlan found himself enjoying the rush. It had been so long since he got to tinker. So long since he got dirty. Something about being in the thick of it all felt reenergizing.

He felt capable. Empowered.

He had relied on other people to take care of the day-to-day for so long, and others to do the coding and creating while he ran a business. He'd forgotten how much fun it was to be hands-on, creating something, solving problems.

Filling the respective areas with gas and oil and checking the air filters, Lachlan confirmed it was the best he could do. He didn't know how long it had been since the last time it was serviced, so he wasn't sure if any of it would make a difference. For all he knew, wires could be damaged, and key parts could be rusted. But at least he tried before they needed it.

He braced himself against another burst of wind and slowly made his way to cottage, now thoroughly drenched from the rain. As he pushed through the door, locking it behind him so the wind wouldn't catch it, he found Charlie waiting for him with a towel.

Her jaw went slack. As much as she tried, she couldn't hide the fact that she was openly gawking at the white, nearly see-through shirt clinging to his body.

Interesting. So maybe this newfound attraction isn't one-sided after all.

He had to know if his theory was right. Lachlan locked eyes with hers and stripped his shirt off slowly, dropping it to the ground. Water droplets ran down the planes of his chest and disappeared into the band of his sweat pants hanging from his hips. Her breath came in fast pants.

"Like what you see?" he goaded, high off her obvious interest.

"I'm...um. Here." She pushed the towel at him, her face turning beet red.

"It's as if you've never seen a half-naked man before," he teased while taking the towel and drying off his hair. "You were conscious last night, weren't you?"

"I was too busy trying not to pass out." She shuddered. "I hate blood, especially mine."

"Charlie," he said in a commanding voice, making her look at him again. When he caught her gaze roving his body involuntarily, he smirked and pointed to his face. "Eyes up here."

"You're such a jerk." She glared at him and lifted her chin. "And for the record, I've seen plenty of naked men in my day."

He raised his eyebrows, a taunting smile still on his face. "Is that so? I didn't know you had it in you. You were always so professional at work."

She folded her arms across her chest. "I didn't mean it like that! I'm just saying, I've had a healthy sex life."

His smile grew.

She shook her head, flustered. "Stop it!"

"Stop what, Charlie?" He took slow steps toward her as if he were a predator on the prowl.

Her green eyes went wide with panic, her face now a deeper red than her hair. She let out a little squeak and half ran, half hobbled up the stairs.

Lachlan laughed, a rumbling sound that filled the empty room. It thrilled him to see her reaction, even if he was messing with her. Something about making her so crazy had him grinning widely, the kind that reached his very soul.

He really liked this Charlie: the uninhibited, honest, *humanized* version of her.

He also *really* liked knowing she might be feeling the same attraction to him as he was for her.

Which was dangerous.

Or fun.

Or a bad idea.

He really didn't know, but as of right now, he was going to savor the fire that coursed through him.

CHAPTER FOURTEEN

MAGICAL BEGINNINGS, my ass.

Charlie stared at herself in the bathroom mirror, fresh-faced from another freezing shower. She brushed her wet hair, trying to figure out if her aunt was playing some kind of practical joke from the Great Beyond. Aunt Violet always did like a good laugh.

Charlie sighed. She missed her.

Wagging a finger at the ceiling, she said, "What do you have up your sleeve, you crazy old lady?"

As expected, there was silence. However, Charlie could imagine Aunt Violet's infectious laughter, the type of cackle she gave when she was up to no good.

The letter had said the cottage was perfect for magic and new beginnings. If that were the case, then why the hell was a man *from her past,* who she was desperate to get away from, trapped in a house with her? A house that sounded like it might blow away with another rough gust of wind.

More importantly, why was Charlie suddenly drawn to him after all these years?

She shook her head. It had to be the setting and situation.

She'd never seen Lachlan thrown into the mix of tough work that didn't require a few clicks of a keyboard. Not that anything was *wrong* with the type of work Lachlan did, per se. However, she'd always been partial to capable men who liked to get their hands dirty.

But seeing him take charge, tending to the house and her wounds...*ugh*. And sharing the bed with him last night, with his rock-hard body pressed against hers...*wow*. She fanned herself just thinking about it. She swore she'd never be one of those women, the ones who practically threw themselves at Lachlan, but her emotions seemed to have other ideas.

All that aside, what really got her was the playful jabs he took a few minutes earlier. The mischievous glint in his eyes. The almost boyish smirk. It was like night and day.

More importantly, was he flirting?

If so, what was she going to do about it?

Her willpower was fading fast. Something about him had her insides fluttering and her lady bits tingling in ways she'd forgotten about. One false move from him, and she might give in.

Which was a *terrible* idea.

Their relationship—or lack thereof—was complicated as it was, and she feared if she crossed that line, he might use it against her.

Like to get her back as his assistant.

Lachlan was strategic, she'd give him that. She'd seen firsthand how he'd get others wrapped around his finger. And even though he had the decency not to bring up the whole reason why he was here again, she knew it was on his mind. He was waiting for the right time to strike.

Maybe when she was vulnerable. Maybe when he'd gained her trust.

She couldn't let that happen. Her head, heart, and hormones all needed to be on the same page. The little glimpse of who he was outside the office couldn't change her whole stance on him. He was a tough boss to work for. He suffocated her with work. She *wouldn't* let that happen again, not after she had her dreams realized and was going for it.

Charlie needed to keep her distance.

A knock sounded at the door. "Hey, Charlie."

She jumped at the sound of his voice, low and sexy. So much for distance. "Yup."

"You almost done in there? I'm full of mud, and the fire isn't doing much to dry my clothes."

Charlie squeezed her eyes shut, doing her best to forget the memories of his shirt clinging to his chiseled body. Or the lustful gleam that filled his eyes when he saw her watching him while he pulled it off.

How could she not look? He was perfect. She almost kicked herself for being too woozy the night before to appreciate his hard, sinewy torso she had been pressed up against.

He'd egged her on a little downstairs, and she couldn't help but wonder if it was honest-to-God teasing or if he was trying to get under her skin for his own benefit.

Charlie opened the door and slipped by him to get to their shared bedroom, her breasts lightly grazing against his chest as she passed by. God, how was she supposed to avoid him if they were living on top of each other?

"Hey," he called out, stopping her in her tracks.

She tentatively turned around and focused her eyes on the ground. "What?"

"How are your cuts?"

Her gaze rose to his, and her defenses waned when she saw the genuine concern reflected there. His voice was soft and caring, making her rational logic from barely seconds before falter.

Charlie held up her hand, now donning a real Band-Aid. "Found some bandages in the deep recesses of my toiletry bag. Can never leave without them, especially if you've got new shoes to break in." She forced a laugh, trying to lighten the mood so she could put separation between them. And fast.

"Right." He leaned against the doorjamb, his chest still bare. She tried to keep her eyes trained on his and not give into the temptation of ogling him again.

She slipped. *Damnit.*

Lachlan's lips pulled up into a slow, panty-melting smile.

"Anyway..." She took a step, trying to retreat to the safety of the bedroom. "I should get changed."

"Got a big day planned?" His voice had that playful, teasing tone to it again. He was up to something.

She stopped and frowned. "Just going to read or something."

Reaching out and taking her elbow before she could escape, Lachlan gently twirled her to face him. "Learning a lot from that book of yours?" he asked, low and dangerous.

She glared at him. Her stomach sank. "What do you mean?"

Oh God, please. No.

"I saw the book poking out from your backpack," he said a little too casually while pushing a wet strand of hair from her face, his fingers featherlight as they moved along her jaw. He was so close that she could feel the warmth of his breath against her chilled skin. A shiver ran through her. "Never took you for the erotica type."

Her face flamed, and she stepped back. "It's not just all sex. There's a story."

He held up his hands in mock defense, the smile still firmly placed on his face. "Hey, no judgment. You surprised me. That's all. You were always so practical and professional. Never would have envisioned you spending your nights reading smut."

This isn't happening.

She waved a hand in front of her, working to regain control of this train wreck of a conversation. "What is this? What's your angle?" She did her best to deflect their conversation. Ideally to a topic that wouldn't make her hope a black hole would magically appear in the floor that she could dive headfirst into. "This isn't you. You don't make jokes. You don't take an interest in others. And you certainly don't invade people's personal space." She lightly slapped his hand away when he twirled another strand of her wet hair around his finger.

Lachlan shrugged one shoulder.

"And you sure as hell aren't casual," she added. "Or smiley. Or *flirty*. What's your deal?"

"Just like your secret dirty book fetish, there's a lot more to me than what meets the eye." He winked, and he strolled into the bathroom, closing the door in her slack-jawed face.

Charlie blew out a breath, now even more disoriented. But when she heard his surprised yell as the hot water turned cold, she couldn't help but feel satisfied.

* * *

The afternoon had been relatively quiet. Aside from Lachlan popping in to grab a change of clothes and to offer her breakfast, he'd been good about leaving her to her thoughts.

Which were about as X-rated as the book she was reading.

Every scene in the book had her imagining Lachlan. After reading had gotten her hot and bothered, she tossed the book aside and threw her arms over her head. Reading was going to be just as dangerous as the man himself.

How the hell did he invade her thoughts so quickly?

Sure, he had always been on her mind in some capacity. Mainly because he never let her think of anything or anyone else. The constant emails, phone calls, and texts with to-dos, requests, and the like had filled her mind and life to the brim. She was his slave. His hostage. But now, thoughts of him had transformed into ones she should never have about her boss.

Ex-boss.

Is this some weird version of Stockholm syndrome?

Another gust of wind and rain pounded against the house, causing the lights to flicker off. She waited a few seconds for them to return as they had done all afternoon. After a minute, she realized they were as good as gone.

"Charlie," Lachlan called up the stairs.

"Yeah?"

"You okay?"

"There's only so much that can happen up here. It's not like the boogeyman appeared in the dark."

"Do I have to remind you of a certain broken window?" he said in the same deep, calculated voice she'd heard so many times at the office. The type of voice that made her feel small.

She frowned, got up, and padded down the hall, sticking her head in the opening to the stairs. "I take it the generator didn't work?"

"It did. Kind of. It has enough juice to handle a room. I figure the kitchen is most important." He rubbed a hand across the back of his neck. "Truthfully, there wasn't much gas to begin with. Not sure how long it will last."

"If the kitchen is fine, why the candle?" She nodded to the lit candle he was holding.

"Conserving generator gas. Would you prefer lights or the fridge? We can get light from the fireplace and these candles. The stove is gas, which doesn't seem to be affected, and we have a wood-burning oven, so that helps. You hungry?"

"No." Her stomach growled.

He cocked his head and smirked. "Charlie Middleton, are you avoiding me?"

She let out an incredulous snort.

"That's what I thought. I'm sure you've had plenty of time alone in that room to think of *all* the reasons why you should stay away. But to keep that beast in your stomach at bay, you may want to reconsider."

Her stomach growled again. "Fine."

He put a hand to his heart. "I promise to be a perfect gentleman."

"Yeah, right." She walked down the stairs and followed him to the kitchen, plopping into a seat at the table.

"Have you heard of me being anything but?"

Charlie laughed. "I guess you're right there. I've seen the trail of broken-hearted women you've left in your wake, and not because you loved 'em and left 'em, but because you wouldn't give them the time of day." She rolled her eyes. "They probably would have died happy if you had even glanced in their direction."

Lachlan shook his head, amused. "Those aren't the kinds of women I want." He disappeared into the pantry, coming out with dry pasta. He pulled out the open jar of sauce from the fridge.

"And what kind of woman does Lachlan Hart want?" She froze. The question had slipped from her lips without her thinking. But it wasn't the intrusive question that petrified her; it was the hope that he'd say it was her.

He looked at her for a beat, making her stomach lurch. His mouth opened and closed as if he was trying to find the right words. Finally, he said, "I really haven't had much time to think about that. The business comes first, always."

Charlie sank back into her chair. That summed up Lachlan completely and gave her the solid reminder that whatever thoughts she had entertained about him were stupid. He would put the company first, before her own career aspirations. Before her heart.

And she wasn't about to have a quick hookup with someone she didn't see a future with. She didn't need a marriage proposal to get into bed with a guy, but she at least wanted some inkling of hope that there could be something more than a booty call, even if it were as simple as a date.

Lachlan's words were loud and clear. He might seem different here in the small confines of the Scottish cottage, but once he got access to the world again, he'd slip away.

"And what kind of man does Charlie Middleton want?" He lit the stovetop with a match and placed a pot of water on the open flame.

Charlie looked down, pulling pieces apart from a paper napkin sitting on the table. "I don't know."

"C'mon. I'm sure you do."

Her gaze shot back up to him. "You think you're the only one who can be too busy with dreams and goals? Don't forget—I was right alongside you, doing the grunt work. If you didn't have time, what makes you think I did?"

Lachlan's good-humored smile fell, his face darkening in the dim light of the kitchen. He turned back to the stove, occupying himself by literally watching water boil.

A pang of guilt hit Charlie right in the gut. She shouldn't have snapped at him like that, even if she was doing it for self-preservation. He didn't know the emotions raging within and the reason she was acting out. It wasn't fair to him, despite the truth of it.

"Lachlan..."

He turned around and stalked to the table. Slapping both hands on it, he leaned in, his face centimeters from hers. She dragged in a shuddering breath, trying her hardest not to close the gap between them.

His lips look so inviting though.

"I'm sorry, Charlie." His voice was quiet and hoarse. The candlelight dancing in his blue eyes rooted her to the spot. "I don't know how many more times I can tell you that I'm sorry for underappreciating you."

He pushed away from the table and pinched the bridge of his nose, his usual tell for when he was frustrated. When he moved is hand away from his face, a range of emotions crossed it. "How can I be better? You know my drive and the reasoning behind it. MindThrive is important to me. To Matteo. My passion for it can't stop. It won't stop. It's all-consuming. And because of it, I can't see beyond it." He ran a hand down his face. "I can't see what else there is for me."

Empathy coursed through her as she saw his vulnerability. Charlie stood slowly and crossed the kitchen. Against her better judgment, she took his hand in hers. The warmth and roughness of it provided unspoken comfort, like she was always meant to have held it. "Nothing you do now will bring me back, Lachlan."

Her stomach twisted. *Why was this suddenly so hard to say?*

His full lips tightened into a thin line. He gave a curt nod. "Regardless, I want to be better. Before you, I had never bothered to understand why I'd lose assistants. Never cared. But your honesty—and the blatant anger behind it—is making me see that I need to do something. If not, I need to understand at least. I need to see it through your eyes."

Charlie softened at that. Lachlan was never the type to look too deeply when things didn't work out. He steamrolled right through issues, finding a replacement or fix as soon as possible. Knowing that about him made her believe she'd be disposable. Once things didn't go his way, he'd discard her and forget everything she did for him.

But now, he was open to understanding. Maybe it wouldn't make him change into a perfect boss, but it was a start.

Maybe it would be a positive beginning for whoever took Charlie's place in his life.

As his assistant.

He entwined their fingers, using his thumb to stroke her soft skin slowly. "Tell me."

Charlie watched his finger trace circles on her hand, electricity coursing through her with each glide of his thumb. He caught her gaze, his eyes slightly hidden by his dark brow. Taking her hand, he slowly lifted it to his mouth, his lips grazing the inside of her wrist with a kiss.

"Wh-what are you doing?" The simple feel of his mouth short-circuited her brain. If a whisper of a kiss could cause that reaction, how would other kisses make her feel?

"I don't know," he answered honestly, now kissing her palm. "Something about you, Charlie, has me feeling...well, I don't really know what I'm feeling. All I know is that being here, with you..." He sighed. "I don't know how I didn't recognize how incredible you are."

She let out a shuddering breath. "So me telling you that you're a terrible boss is what does it for you?" She tried to make the joke, but her shaky voice lacked amusement.

He smiled against the top of her hand as he kissed it again and placed it back to her side while letting go. She resisted the urge to grab it again.

"Well, I'm pretty impressed that you laid it all out there. Most people wouldn't. Seems like they hold back around me."

"They do. They're intimidated." Her pulse was still going crazy as she tried to wrap her head around the shift in conversation.

He cocked his head. "Why? It's not like I go off the handle when things don't go my way."

"You don't have to shout to make people nervous. You have a certain way about you. Quiet. Pensive. We never know what you're really thinking. And then there's that stare." Lachlan's eyes bored into hers. "Yeah. Like that. I feel like you could see right through me." She shifted uncomfortably.

"I'm just inside my head, trying to process what's said or work through a problem. Most of the time I'm not registering what's in front of me. I'm thinking."

"I see." She turned to pour two glasses of wine.

The more she talked to Lachlan, the more she started to understand the man who seemed hidden to the world.

And the more she liked it.

Yes, he was passionate about his work to a fault. But he wasn't cold, calculated, and purposely distant as she once believed. He felt like the world was on his shoulders and didn't have the support anymore to help him handle the weight. Matteo was mostly out of the picture.

Lachlan couldn't miss a beat. Everything fell on him. The decisions. The problems. The opportunities. If he made one small error in judgment, all of it could be gone. Charlie shuddered, thinking about that kind of pressure. If she felt he was tough on her, she would have never been able to handle the high-level expectations he placed on himself.

That the world placed on him.

"Lachlan, I—" She turned, finding him so near that it startled her.

The look in his eyes was a mix of burden, understanding...and lust.

He cupped her face, tracing his thumb along her jawline and down her throat, and took a deep breath. "It's been a while since I had this level of honest conversation with someone. Since Matteo."

Goose bumps pricked her skin where he touched her. Her heart raced when she realized he had started to let her into his world—a world only reserved for the very few, the very special.

Lachlan's fingertips traced her bottom lip. "Since I saw you when I arrived here, I've wanted to know what this feels like. I can't stop thinking about it." His whisper sent shivers down her spine.

Her heart pounded harder, thumping so violently against her ribs she thought they might crack.

Oh my God, Lachlan Hart is going to kiss me.

He let out a soft groan as she licked her lips.

"I want you to," she whispered back.

A flash of relief crossed his face as if he were hanging on her answer. As if how she responded would make or break him. A look of lust and longing made his eyes grow dark and mysterious as he took in a deep breath. He lowered his head slowly, and Charlie wrapped her arms around his neck, bringing him closer. The feel of her breasts pushing against his hard chest made her knees go weak.

She wanted more. The anticipation was killing her.

Lachlan circled his arms around her waist and pulled her against him. His growing erection against her stomach made her throb. She damn near came undone before he even put his lips on her.

He dipped his head down, his mouth only a breath from hers. Charlie's eyes fluttered closed, feeling light-headed from the excitement. The need.

How could she have ever thought she could stay away from him?

But before their lips met, her eyes flashed open. She pushed away. "Did you hear that?"

Lachlan blinked, his reaction slightly delayed. His eyebrows knitted in confusion. "Hear what?" She could see the disappointment on his face. If his sexual frustration was anywhere near hers right now, she could understand.

Charlie rushed to the front door and pulled it open, bringing in a gust of wind and rain. In the distance, she heard it again.

A bark.

"I think that's the grocer's dog. She ran away before the storm."

Lachlan still stood in the doorway of the kitchen, likely stunned by her complete one-eighty. "Are you sure? He didn't find her?"

"Not the last time I talked to him."

"What wildlife is out there, Charlie? Could it be a wolf or coyote?"

"That bark is like no wolf I've heard." The dog barked and whined once more, this time sounding scared. It tugged at her heart. She slipped on her shoes and pulled open the door farther.

"What do you think you're doing?" Lachlan's long legs allowed him to cross the room in a couple of steps, but not fast enough to stop her.

"I'm going to find her!" Charlie shouted over the raging storm and exploded out the front door.

She raced into the darkness. Without electricity to light the streetlamps, it was almost impossible to see through the sideways rain. But she wasn't going to let that dog suffer all alone in the storm. She couldn't. Following the sound of the dog's barks, Charlie crossed the road and ran-walked up the hill. The streets were slick with wet leaves and fallen branches, making it hard to get traction.

She pushed wet hair away from her face. Within a matter of seconds, she was soaked to the bone. Her clothes felt like weights that threatened to slam her down and hold her to the ground. Another powerful gust of wind knocked Charlie to her knees. Pain radiated up her leg to match the pain in her foot from last night.

"Charlie! Where are you?" Lachlan shouted in the distance.

Another whimper up ahead put her on high alert. She moved quickly toward it, getting farther away from the safety of the cottage.

And Lachlan.

CHAPTER FIFTEEN

"CHARLIE! DAMN IT!" Lachlan's roar was barely audible over the unrelenting rain. Overwhelming darkness made impossible to see a few yards ahead. The torrent of wind and rainfall muffled out any other noise. He'd never hear her if she called out for him.

His shoe slid in thick mud, and he teetered a moment before righting himself. A flash of lightning streamed across the sky, providing just enough light to see down the road. The water had risen to the main strip and was now slowly creeping up the bottom of Queen Mary's Alley. He prayed Charlie didn't run into the rising water. Not only could it sweep her away, but downed power lines could be hidden underneath.

She'd be dead in a heartbeat if one of them was live.

Lachlan called out for her again, his panic increasing when he heard nothing back. His chest rose and fell rapidly as he trudged up the hill, trying his hardest to find her.

Why didn't I think to bring a flashlight?

Probably because he was acting out of instinct. The woman he cared for had raced into the night, disregarding the dangers lurking beyond the safe confines of the cottage. Out here, he could tell the storm was picking up. The house already was rattling as it was. Could it take much more?

A crack of lightning flashed again. He could see movement ahead, but couldn't be sure if it was Charlie or a tall bush whipping in the wind. He picked up his pace, running up the hill, chasing after the fleeting image. As he was about to take another step, a gust of wind knocked him down. He landed hard on his back, losing his breath in the process.

Stunned and a little sore, he took a second to get his bearings. He tried to push himself up, but the powerful wind made it nearly impossible.

Dread coursed through him, his stomach clenching. If he was having this much trouble, how was Charlie fairing? She was at least half a foot shorter than him and didn't have the same mass he did. If he could get tossed around so easily, she could be seriously hurt.

"Charlie!" Nearly drowned by the rain, he sputtered, coughing out water that went down the wrong pipe.

Lachlan pulled himself up and pushed ahead. Her life depended on him.

"Lachlan!"

He whipped around, searching for the faint calling of his name, trying his hardest to hear it again.

Nothing.

His body tensed. What if she was hurt? What if he couldn't get to her in time? He shouted for her again, his fear making it sound desperate. Broken.

"Lachlan!"

It was closer this time, but more alarmed. He raced blindly toward it, slipping on loose stones and mud. He lost his balance as a fallen branch tripped him, but he managed to stay upright.

A flash overhead illuminated the area, outlining Charlie's silhouette a couple of houses away. Relief flooded through him. She was drenched but unscathed. Battling the storm as he moved closer, he could make out a shivering dog lying on the ground. He ran to them.

"Are either of you hurt?"

"No. I think she's just scared."

"Stay where you are," he ordered as another roar of thunder came, rumbling so loudly, it made his teeth chatter. Only a few more yards, and he'd be right there with her.

Charlie bent down, coaxing the dog to stand. The dog, with long red hair that reminded him of Charlie, tentatively licked her hand but wouldn't stand up. From Lachlan's vantage point, he could see the thing was trembling uncontrollably.

"I think we're going to have to carry her," she said over another clap of thunder. "I can't lift her."

"I'll get her. Just stay put."

He mumbled under his breath about how insane she was for running out in a storm like this for an animal she didn't even know. She was putting them all at risk, but damn if his heart didn't squeeze a little when he saw how gentle she was with the frightened animal.

A stream of lightning filled the sky. Its spidery veins reached down and hit a tree next to Charlie. A thick limb splintered and came crashing down.

"Charlie!" He dug in, trying to close the last bit of distance between them. The slick street and mud made him feel like he was running in place.

He couldn't see her. Couldn't hear her.

Fuck! Charlie.

CHAPTER SIXTEEN

CHARLIE FELT Lachlan's hands before she saw him kneeling beside her. Stunned from the near miss, she lay in a pile of mud next to a fallen tree limb.

"Are you okay?" His voice was muffled like he was underwater.

She shook, trying to pull herself from a dazed state. "I'm okay"". The dog?" She scrambled to her knees to search.

"The dog's fine. Just scared."

Even in the dark, Charlie could see his intense stare. His eyebrows knitted, a look he usually gave when he wasn't pleased, but a flash of something else crossed his face: worry.

She reached out and cupped his jaw—a mix of slickness from the rain and roughness from his thickening scruff.

Lachlan grabbed her wrist, pulling her from her stupor. "We have to go."

As if to punctuate his sense of urgency, another earth-shattering rumble startled them, followed by a bright flash. He whistled to the dog, but the poor thing wouldn't move.

"You're going to have to carry her," Charlie yelled over the whipping wind. "We had a dog like this growing up. Terrified of storms."

Lachlan pinched the bridge of his nose and cursed. He crouched down and allowed the sweet girl to sniff his hand. After the dog gave a tiny lick, he scooped her up, throwing her over one of his broad shoulders.

He turned to Charlie and reached out. "Take my hand."

Charlie slipped her hand into his, feeling it envelop hers like he was clutching on to the last shred of hope. At a carefully slow pace, they continued down the small hill leading to the cottage. During the short walk, they nearly toppled over twice from the wind gusts, and Charlie cried out when a bolt of lightning hit the ground nearby.

They finally made it to the cottage, soaked to the bone and covered in mud. Lachlan pushed through the front door, pulling her with him before he closed it with force and locked it. He crossed the room and placed the nervous retriever on the wooden floor near the fireplace. The dog wasted no time shaking herself with everything she had, spraying them both with more water and mud. Satisfied, the dog made a few circles and nestled near the warmth from the fire.

Charlie shivered from the cold wetness that seemed to seep straight to her bones. "Well, I guess she's made herself at home," she said, breaking the silence between them.

He turned to face her, his chest heaving with deep, harsh breaths. His T-shirt clung to his muscles, causing a new shiver to run through her.

"What were you thinking?" he growled in a quiet whisper, his body tense.

His gaze locked on hers, rooting her to the spot like they had done so many times before. With the light from the fire dancing in them, they looked sinister in the dark room. His nostrils flared as he let out a frustrated breath. Gone was the man she had started to know these last couple of days. The one who could smile. The one who could tease and flirt.

The old Lachlan was back with a vengeance.

"I'm sorry. I wasn't thinking—"

"No. You weren't."

She flinched at the way he spat out the words like she was a reckless idiot. "You don't have to come down on me like that. I said I was sorry."

He crossed the room in two strides, leaving barely an inch between them. Her chest grazed across his every time she took a breath. Taking a step back, Charlie found herself pressed against the wall. Lachlan closed in on her, placing his palms on the wall, caging her in.

"You don't understand, Charlie. You could have been killed. Both of us could have died out there." He towered over her. Crowded her.

"I—"

Before she could finish her thought, Lachlan took her face in both of his hands—a mixture of rough and gentle as if trying to restrain himself—and pushed the wet hair from her temple to behind her ear. "I was scared, Charlie. I was scared something could have happened to you." His voice was thick with emotion.

She sucked in a breath. The anger in his eyes had morphed into something more. Fear. Affection.

Lust.

His gaze flicked down to her lips, and at that moment, there was nothing more she wanted than to give in to him.

As if sensing her desire, Lachlan delivered.

"Charlie." Her name died on his tongue as he bent down to her, crushing his lips against hers.

Lachlan pushed her slowly against the wall, using it as leverage. She wrapped her arms around his neck and combed her fingers through his wet hair, tugging gently.

His lips—full and solid, yet soft—matched her own, kissing as if he knew exactly what she wanted. She opened her mouth to let his tongue explore, meeting hers in an erotic dance that made her moan.

Lachlan's breathing was ragged. She could tell he was losing the battle of self-control with each stroke of their tongues. He moved his hands from her face, down her neck and collarbone, and skimmed the side of her breasts and ribs. He grabbed her hips, pulling her firmly against his hard body, nipping and kissing his way down her neck and to the sensitive spot behind her ear. "I couldn't bear the thought of losing you," he whispered in between kisses.

She pulled his head back up so she could kiss him again, putting everything she could into it. Never in her life would she have expected this, but now that it was here, she couldn't think of a single thing she wanted more.

Her legs went weak, her bones turned into jelly. She was drunk off his kiss, light-headed from the high of it. There was a fire burning in the pit of her stomach, moving lower.

She needed him. More of him. All of him.

Lachlan pulled away and pressed his forehead against hers. They sucked in air, an impossible task when they both were breathing like they'd run a marathon. "I'm sorry," he said, their harsh breaths mingling together.

"For what?" Her voice was husky and raw. She dug her fingers into his hair, holding him to her. She wasn't ready for this to end. Whatever *this* was.

"For kissing you like that. You've...you've gotten under my skin."

Charlie pulled away and raised an eyebrow. "That's not usually a good thing."

Lachlan kissed her forehead and smiled. "I mean it in the best, most confusing way possible. Since I arrived here, I haven't been able to stop thinking about you."

"Not hard. You're stuck in a thousand-square-foot structure with me, the only woman on this whole island."

He shook his head and held her face in his hands, his blue eyes gleaming in the dim light. "It's not that, Charlie. I feel like I'm seeing you for the first time. And..."

"And what?" she asked with breathless hope.

"And I've been dying to kiss you. Needed it. I've tried to keep my distance, but seeing you out there and thinking you were crushed under that tree...I didn't want to waste another moment."

His eyes were earnest, a look unusual for Lachlan, but one she found sexy as hell. She felt a connection to him that seemed impossible to forge through the three years she'd worked for him. She was seeing the human side to him, and damned if it wasn't heart-stopping.

"It's okay. I...I liked it. Loved it," she said.

His serious expression relaxed a fraction.

"This might make things more complicated," he started to say as she pushed the wet, dark hair away from his forehead. He took one of her hands and kissed it. "Your hands are freezing."

"Makes sense. I'm frozen."

"Right. We need to get changed." He guided her up the stairs and into the bathroom.

"What are we doing?" she asked, nerves and anticipation making her voice shake.

"I need to see you in the light. I want to make sure you didn't get hurt out there." He lit the candles he had placed on the vanity earlier and held one up to her.

"A branch clipped me. But I think I'm okay."

After putting a candle back on the vanity, he carefully removed the bandage from her hand. "Your cuts from yesterday are full of dirt. We need to get you cleaned up."

Charlie simply nodded, overwhelmed with emotion. How he managed to go from giving her the hottest kiss of her life to treating her with such tenderness was a shock to her system. If her feelings for him were messy before, they were even messier now. Was he still here to persuade her to work for him again?

Whatever his intentions, how could she convince herself to keep her distance from a man who clearly cared for her and her well-being? It was a fight she didn't want to do anymore, even if she'd regret it. Giving in to him—even for a night—would make it that much harder to keep her resolve about her resignation.

Lachlan turned on the faucet and eased her hand under the stream of cool water. "Where did you get hit? Did you hurt your foot again?"

Charlie looked at his reflection in the mirror. His forehead was scrunched in concentration as he tended to her. She never thought he'd have that level of focus for anything other than his work. But here he was, putting every ounce of his attention on making sure she was safe.

"My foot feels sore but okay. The branch hit my right side. Shoulder and rib."

Lachlan turned off the water and released her hand. "Can I take a look?" He swallowed. Hard. He was asking permission to see her body.

Even if it was purely to assess an injury, warmth pooled low in her belly.

"Yes." She moved into the burning candle's faint light.

Lachlan's breath came deep but steady. He reached for the bottom of her shirt and slowly pulled up. The damp cloth stuck to her skin peeled away, revealing her body to the cool air in the room. He watched every inch that became exposed like it was a comet that only passed Earth once every few hundred years. If he blinked, he might miss it.

He brushed his hands along her bare skin, pushing the shirt over the swells of her breasts, and finally over her head. Charlie stood there in her black bra before him. She felt like her heart might explode at the way his darkened gaze trailed up and down her body. A strand of his hair fell across his forehead, and her hand itched to reach out and push it aside. To linger there and feel the warmth of his skin against her palm.

Moving closer, Lachlan traced his rough fingers along her ribs where a bruise was starting to form. Charlie sucked in a breath, making him pull his hand away. "I didn't mean to hurt you."

Should she tell him it wasn't the bruise that had stopped her breathing, but the feel of his hands on her?

Lachlan grabbed a towel and draped it over her shoulders with hesitation, seemingly reluctant to cover her body. A body his eyes were feasting on just a second before. "You should get some dry clothes," he murmured. "You don't want to get sick."

Charlie nodded and left the bathroom wordlessly, worried that if she spoke, she might suggest continuing the kiss from downstairs.

And if they started again, she knew she wouldn't be able to stop.

* * *

After they had both had cleaned off and changed into dry clothes, Charlie tiptoed down the stairs. She paused halfway and took in the scene. There, in front of the fire, was the outline of Lachlan's broad form stroking the dog. The dog, thankful for his compassion, scooted closer and rested her head on his outstretched legs. He placed a soft kiss on her head, and she let out a content sigh.

He had also brought down some pillows and blankets, making for a cozy slumber party by the fire.

Her heart squeezed. Something about seeing this private moment made her believe she was seeing the man Lachlan really was. In fact, everything about how he'd been since arriving to the island tested what she knew about him. He might have come with his own agenda —to bring her back as his assistant—but he hadn't pushed the issue. Instead, he rolled up his sleeves and helped out. He ensured the house was in its best condition for the storm, took care of her injuries, saved her from a fallen tree, and gave her the only good bed in the house.

And he kissed her with feeling, giving her a little more of himself. There was raw passion behind it. She could feel it. But what did it all mean?

"Hey," she said as she walked down the rest of the stairs and took a seat next to him. She rubbed her hands together and stretched them toward the fire. "I feel like I'll never get warm."

Lachlan mindlessly stroked the dog's ears. "I can grab you another blanket from upstairs."

Charlie smiled. "I wouldn't want to disturb the girl. She's been through a lot. Seems like she's in good hands now though."

He nodded. "Yeah. She's a well-loved dog. I can tell. Is it the same one as your grocer friend's?"

"From the picture I saw, looks like it. Same beautiful red coat." Charlie reached over to pet the dog. "Hm. What's this?" she asked as she felt under the retriever's thick fur. "She's got a collar." Charlie leaned down, resting her torso on Lachlan's legs as she got closer to the tag. "Her name is Nessie. It's definitely his dog. His information is on the backside."

A low laugh rumbled through Lachlan. "Nessie. Guess he's a Loch Ness Monster believer."

Charlie pushed up to sit. "Hey, there are stranger things in life."

He shot her a sidelong glance. "Like the two of us being stranded on a deserted island in a cottage that may or may not weather this storm?"

She grinned. "Yeah, something like that. Or the fact that I haven't killed you yet," she drawled and let out a sigh. "This wasn't at all what I expected when I came here."

"The things you need in life never are. Just like how I never expected one algorithm would shape my whole future."

"Pretty deep for you." She knocked her shoulder against his.

He shrugged and smirked. "What do you think I do all that time when I'm being standoffish, like you pointed out? I can't busy myself with small talk *and* come up with these profound statements."

They both watched the fire in companionable silence for a moment, enjoying the warmth it provided. "Charlie," Lachlan finally said.

"Hmm?"

"What's your real name?"

She turned to him with a confused smile. "What do you mean? It's Charlie."

"Is it short for something? I've wondered. Charlotte maybe?"

She shook her head. "Just Charlie. Named after my father. I never met him." She focused on the fire. "It's all very complicated. I don't want to bore you."

"You said I never took the time to get to know you. Well, now I am. It might be too little, too late. But I'm here to listen if you want to share."

Charlie exhaled, moved by the openness in his voice. Maybe all they had was this island together, and once they left, they'd go their separate ways. But opening up to him felt right.

"His name was Charlie Knight. He died in a car accident before my mom could ever tell him she was pregnant." She gave him a quick glance from the corner of her eye. His steady gaze and encouraging smile made her comfortable enough to continue sharing. "From what my mom told me, they were insanely in love. After him, she swore she would never find something that came close to that again. Truthfully, she must have believed it because I don't think I'd ever seen her with another man. Charlie Knight was the only one for her.

"My mom says I get my curiosity and determination from him. He was going to go to school to be a marine biologist. He wanted to know all the secrets of the ocean." She smiled at that.

"So your parents were in high school then?"

"Yeah. Mom's life wasn't easy because of it. Growing up in the Bible Belt, it was a huge deal that she was not only a pregnant seventeen-year-old, but also that she'd had premarital sex. Apparently, both sets of my grandparents were fiercely religious."

"You say that as if you don't know for yourself."

Charlie leaned back and used her hands to prop her up. Her pinky finger rubbed the side of Lachlan's hand resting nearby, and the small contact sent electricity up her arm. "Because I don't. My mother's parents disowned her. My father's parents wanted nothing to do with her. Religion is supposed to teach you love and forgiveness. For my mom, the Commandments or rules or whatever were something my grandparents lived by. They chose that over the love for their own daughter."

"I'm sorry, Charlie."

"My aunt Violet and uncle Jon took my mom in. My grandparents basically shunned my aunt too for accepting my mother and her 'sin'—that's me if you haven't gathered. Anyway, the three of them were all I had for family. Now it's just my mom and me."

"I never would have known."

She lifted a shoulder. "And why would you? Maybe my family life was untraditional, but they loved me very much. That's why I'm so set on *not* coming back to work for you." His body tensed. "My mother did everything she could to make sure I have the opportunities she never had. She dropped out of high school to have me and worked odd jobs to support us. She only went back to school to get her degree so she could become a teacher when I reached high school. She put her whole life on hold for me, and she didn't do that just so I could take care of someone else while they built their own dreams." She said the last part with a little more force than needed.

A mixture of amusement, understanding, and appreciation crossed Lachlan's features. And dare she say, respect? He stared at her as if seeing her for the first time. Saying nothing, he gave a tight nod while he absorbed it all. Something flashed quickly across his face, as if he were fighting an internal battle.

"What is it?" Charlie asked.

He slid his hand closer to hers and held it. Her heart thumped hard at the small but impactful gesture. "I guess I'm inspired by you. How you're confident in your decision to go after what you want, even if it means a huge life change."

She laughed softly. "I'm terrified, Lach. I'd hoped coming here would help me find some perspective and make me feel like I'm making the right decision. I think I am, but it's all so different. What if it's not what I expected? What if I'm not good at it?"

"Did you find it? The perspective?"

She rested her head on his shoulder, watching the fire dance in the hearth. "There's no clear answer, at least not the one I thought I'd magically find here. But there's one thing I'm positive about, and it's that I'll never know if I don't put myself out there and try. I owe it to myself to try. I have the drive and the opportunity to do it, so why not? Why not see what's out there for me? The only thing that would stop me is *me*. Nothing else. I just need to get out of my own way."

Lachlan placed a kiss on her head, pausing to nestle his face in her hair and breathe in. "You're right." He sighed. "More than you realize."

CHAPTER SEVENTEEN

EARLY THE NEXT MORNING, Lachlan woke to find Charlie in his arms, her cheek resting on his chest, and Nessie curled against his back. At some point, they had all fallen asleep in front of the fireplace.

Yet despite how uncomfortable the unforgiving wood floors were, he didn't want to move.

There was truth to what Charlie had said about him. He put everything he had into his work, and other areas of his life suffered because of it. Relationships—or lack thereof—and tapping into his other passions were two glaring ones that came to mind.

Hell, he wasn't even sure if he had any other passions anymore. He never gave himself a moment to think of what else was out there. Everything was about MindThrive AI.

For a while, there had been a nagging desire in the back of his mind. One that told him it was time to consider new opportunities. That it was *okay* to branch out and find something that sparked the same fire within him MindThrive had years ago. Right before Matteo's accident, he was going to go for it.

But with Matteo out of the equation, Lachlan knew it wasn't an option. And as much as that voice still pestered him, he had found a way to ignore it.

Now he was wondering what silencing that desire had cost him.

As Charlie wriggled against him to get more of his warmth, his insides squeezed. How was such an amazing woman like her right in front of him this whole time and he never noticed? The way she passionately spoke about taking chances, despite her fears, had him in absolute awe.

When was the last time he took a chance?

For the past few years, his focus had been about making the right choices so the company could not only survive, but also thrive. He was, after all, a man of logic. Every decision was scrutinized and chosen based on his in-depth market research. And more importantly, what the investors would believe in the most to fund.

His company had been a passion project with Matteo. They pushed the limits because, in their eyes, there were no limits. The only thing that could hold them back from creating was how little their minds could imagine. That kind of thinking was how MindThrive AI even came to be.

But he couldn't recall the last time he was energized about something like he had been those years working with Matteo in their apartment. Or the last time he'd tested how far his imagination could take him to develop something new. Hell, he couldn't even remember how long it had been since he actually wrote code for himself.

In the early years of the company, he would sit with the developers and peer program with them. He had more freedom and time to get into the thick of things instead of being bogged down with the details of the business or meetings that never seemed to end. He nearly rolled his eyes, thinking of the buzzword bingo in all those dry presentations.

Back then, it had been all about creating something revolutionary. Lachlan had been more connected to the company and its people. He'd mentored them, helped them grow in their own careers. He had felt like he was one of them, not dissociated like he was now.

He'd had more passion too.

Yes, he was still devoted to the company and what they did, but something about it made him feel empty and aimless. He worked as a means of survival. Not for him, because he had enough money to float on for the rest of his life if he retired, but for everyone else. For Matteo and his family. For the employees who relied on him. For keeping the dream that he and Matteo had alive. For protecting what they built.

It was no longer about creating. No longer about discovery.

Being here with Charlie had somehow made him see that. It also made him realize how other areas of his life were lacking. Maybe she didn't find the perspective she had hoped for when coming to the Isle of Murdina, but he was starting to.

And it was a little scary.

As Charlie stirred, he realized another thing since coming to the island: his life didn't feel right without her in it. At first, he thought it had to do with her impeccable skills at keeping his life on track. So much so that he went the lengths of jumping on a plane across the Atlantic to convince her to come back.

But now he knew it went beyond that. *Way* beyond that. He wanted to be with her, and the thought scared the shit out of him, yet not as much as the idea of being without her.

Charlie reminded him of what could be. Hearing her story last night and seeing the fire in her eyes to chase after what she wanted seeped into the depths of him. Something that went dormant long ago was shifting. Awakening.

The feeling that something was missing these last few years was now starting to make sense. He didn't know what it was yet, but he knew he was on the verge of something big because of her.

He swallowed hard. As he thought of it more, he started to remember what that feeling was.

Change.

He was on the brink of change. What that change was, he wasn't sure. But it was time. Something had to give. He couldn't continue living a life where he wasn't connected to what he was doing anymore. Or connected to anyone, for that matter.

That was another thing Charlie had shown him. He not only needed more meaningful human connection, but he also craved it. Specifically, from her. Being around her made him feel lighter, engaged, and hopeful. He wanted to go beyond himself. He wanted to look up and see what was around him. He wanted to take care of her the way she had done for him all these years.

When they went back to New York, he wanted her in his life. Somehow. Some way.

How could a couple of days change so much for him?

"Lach?" Her voice was a sleepy whisper. She craned her neck and looked over her shoulder with one eye open. Her red hair—now crazy waves from sleeping on it wet—cascaded down her back when she shifted. "Did we fall asleep on the floor?"

"Seems so."

Charlie opened her other eye. She scanned their current situation, seeing how her body fit against his and the fact that his arm was snaked around her middle, holding her secure against him. She closed her eyes again, a lazy smile filling her face.

Then her eyes popped open, her horrified look washing away the smile he was growing to love. She shifted so their bodies were no longer touching and sat up.

"I didn't mean to." She stumbled over her words as she hugged her pillow like it was a defensive shield.

Lachlan propped his head on his hand and grinned. "You didn't do anything. It just happened."

"I know, but this," she said while pointing a finger back and forth between them, "is already complicated as it is. You said so yourself. First, you coming here. And then the kiss." She almost moaned the word and then shook her head. "It's all very confusing."

"Because you shouldn't kiss your boss?" He tugged her hair.

She glared at him, her green eyes turning into the same angry slits from when he first arrived. "I hope you're not pushing that issue again. I thought I made it clear on where we stood with that."

He flopped onto his back, interlocked his fingers, and cradled his head in his hands. "I was teasing, Charlie. Relax. I heard you loud and clear." And he was no longer here for that. He didn't want her as his assistant. He just wanted *her.* "Was trying to lighten the mood since you seemed so stressed about some innocent spooning."

"What I felt pressed against my back was *not* innocent."

Lachlan's hearty laugh echoed through the small room. "You must not have realized you were rubbing yourself up against it before you woke up." He sat up and held up his hands in surrender. "I was helpless."

She threw a pillow at him. "You're lying!"

He caught her wrists before she grabbed more ammo and held her there. Cocking his head to the side, he taunted, "I think your subconscious is acting out those books you're reading."

"Shut up," she said, flustered with no comeback. Her cheeks flushed to a pretty tinge of pink.

"Unless you were dreaming about something else. *Someone* else." He couldn't help but wind her up. When her face turned twenty shades darker, he knew he had hit the jackpot. A part of Lachlan hoped she was thinking of him.

She tossed another pillow at him and stood. "I should shower. Or take the dog out. Or make breakfast," she rattled off, still clearly embarrassed and trying to find anything to get away from him.

"Hey," Lachlan said softly as he stood too. He put his hands on her shoulders to keep her from running off. "I was just giving you a hard time."

Charlie raised her sheepish gaze to meet his. "I'm not saying you're wrong, but…"

Lachlan burst out laughing. *Interesting.*

She shook off his hands and crossed her arms. "You think you can kiss me the way you did last night and I wouldn't dream about it?"

He lifted an eyebrow. "So you're admitting I'm the man of your dreams?"

She snorted. "I wouldn't go that far." He might have believed her if he didn't catch the small smile playing on her lips.

What was it about her that made him feel so lighthearted and eager to have fun? Even in their shitty situation. Even after missing a major meeting with the investors. Even challenging everything he worked for these last few years.

Waking up to Charlie had put him in a good mood. The best mood. And he wanted to hold on to the feeling for as long as he could.

He thought of all those long days at the office with her. Maybe if he had just looked up and saw her there, things wouldn't have felt so hard on him. Even if it were a glance, the brief vacation from the insurmountable pressure would have been enough.

He moved his hands down her arms and grabbed her hips lightly. "I took a transatlantic flight for you. Saved you from danger. Twice. Cooked for you. Gave you the good blanket. That's not 'Dream Man' worthy?" He scooped her up in his arms, eliciting a surprised squeak from her.

"Lachlan, what are you doing?" She laughed, a sound that sparked his soul. A sound he wanted to listen to forever.

He paused to memorize the crinkle of her faintly freckled nose and the way one side of her smile rose higher than another. These were the details he wanted to always remember about her.

He had it bad.

"Clearly you have high expectations. Maybe if I carry you around like a princess? Dote on you? Will that finally be enough to make me the man of your dreams?"

Her laughter stopped. A soft grin was still on her lips, but her eyes had gone serious. Introspective. She searched his face as if honestly considering his question, pausing on his lips for a second too long. All playing had disappeared and was now replaced with the same heat he had felt when he'd kissed her last night.

He wanted her again. Needed to taste her. To feel her full mouth against his. To hear her soft moan coming from the deep recesses of her body, calling for him.

Maybe his breathing stopped. Or maybe it was hers. Or maybe it was both of theirs. But he could see his own want reflected in her eyes. They had said taking this any further than platonic would be complicated. And it would be.

But he couldn't remember why. Didn't care.

Charlie absentmindedly licked her lips, which only made them look that much more enticing. He wanted to follow that trail with his tongue. Against his better judgment, he leaned closer to her. Her eyes fluttered shut, waiting for him to close the gap between them.

And that's when the house shook.

Startled, Lachlan nearly dropped her.

Nessie jumped to her feet, letting out a scared whimper.

Charlie wrapped her arms tighter around his neck as he righted her. "What the hell was that?"

Another shake was followed by a loud crash.

Lachlan put her on the ground and took her hand, leading them up the stairs to their bedroom window. Nessie scurried behind them closely, not daring to let them leave her sight. Standing behind Charlie, Lachlan's chest pressed against her back as they peered out. Sparks lit up the sky.

"Looks like more transformers are blowing because..." He squinted harder. "Because the water is rising up the road. I think the power lines are in the water."

Charlie tensed against him. "It's already been a full day of this. How much worse can it get?"

He wrapped his arm around her shoulders and placed a kiss in her hair. "I don't know."

"I thought you said we'd be safe from the storm surge up here."

Lachlan sucked in a breath. "I didn't want to tell you because I didn't want you to worry, but I think it was a full moon last night. That changes the tides. Makes things worse."

"Do you think it will make it up here? The water is only a few houses away now."

"I think we'll be okay. I hope we will be."

Selfishly, he wanted to be right. He wanted to make it off the island and back to New York so they could explore whatever it was going on between them. Somewhere normal. Safe. Realistic. He wanted to believe there was more to his feelings than the adrenaline of being in a place that was foreign and dangerous.

And if it was, he wanted to show Charlie that too.

CHAPTER EIGHTEEN

CHARLIE LAY in bed that afternoon—alone—with a book to pass the time. But the words were white noise to the thoughts and feelings churning within her.

That kiss. The intensity of Lachlan's stare, this time full of desire instead of disappointment. The way he seemed different on the island. A bit conflicted, but somehow unburdened.

Lachlan might have joked about all he'd done for her while here, but Charlie couldn't deny the fact that it rang true. He took care of her. He made her feel safe. What if she let go and gave into whatever was brewing between them? Would that still be the case if it weren't just the two of them stuck in this odd circumstance? Would he go back to workaholic mode where she was left juggling everything to make his life easier?

She shook her head and rolled over, shoving her face on the pillow to stifle a scream. There was no "what if." There was Lachlan Hart, the tech genius who put his work before all, and there was Charlie Middleton, a woman determined to make her own career without any distractions.

And a distraction, Lachlan was.

The flirtation and kiss might seem innocent here where there weren't any *actual* consequences. But what happened when the real world interrupted their safe little bubble?

Would he try to get her to come back to work for him? If not, would he treat their relationship like she was his assistant for his personal life? Old habits were hard to break. She'd seen people fall back into the same cycles, the dynamics of the relationships reverting to old patterns.

Could she really avoid him if he kept touching her the way he has? Kept giving her his playful smile, making the laugh lines deepen around his eyes that twinkled with mischief whenever he teased her? Had she met him at a different time, in a different situation, she could see herself falling hard and fast for him.

But they had history, and this brief break from the realities of their lives wasn't forever.

Pretty soon, those sparkling eyes will become sharp and emotionless again. His playful jabs at her would be short, curt, to-the-point conversational points. Nothing more. Nothing less. And he sure as hell wouldn't kiss her with the heat he had last night. Chances were, they would never cross each other's paths again now that she'd left MindThrive AI.

The thought depressed her.

How was it that barely a week ago, she was desperate to get away from him? And now, she hated the thought of not seeing him?

The sound of Lachlan's curse traveled upstairs.

"What's wrong?" she asked as she made her way down, finding him stoking the fireplace. Nessie watched him with interest, her tail thumping against the floor.

"The generator went down."

"From the storm, or is it out of gas?"

Wind slammed tree branches against the house. Nessie whimpered and scurried to Lachlan's side for safety.

"Not feeling up to going outside to find out. Either way, we have officially lost electricity."

"Food?"

"We have nonperishable stuff, so we're okay there. But it's dwindling. We're nearly bare bones here. If we can't get off this island in another couple of days, we're going to be out." He crouched down to the dog to scratch behind her ears. "I hope you don't mind, but I gave her the last of the lunch meat. I wasn't sure when she last ate."

Charlie melted at his concern for Nessie. "That's fine."

Another gust of wind had the house groaning in ways she hadn't heard before. Lachlan stood and stilled, listening to the unnatural sounds of the cottage. "That doesn't sound right."

The house felt like it was shaking in the wind. Charlie imagined it blowing off its foundation and spinning around midair like in *The Wizard of Oz*. Only, there would be no safe landing in a colorful place full of interesting characters.

A consistent banging sounded against the outer side of the kitchen. "What the hell is that?"

Lachlan listened. "I think...it sounds like rocks slamming against each other."

As if to confirm his suspicions, a gray stone from the fence flew through the kitchen window, breaking through the boards they had put up for protection.

Charlie screamed and gripped on to Lachlan, frozen against his sturdy frame. The cottage that had felt safe to her was now breached. Whatever hope she had for weathering this storm vanished. As she stared at the stone and splintered wood sitting on the kitchen floor, she feared they might not make it through.

"Does this mean the storm is getting worse? To pull a stone from the fence like that and break the wood means it had to have some force."

Lachlan looked down at her, concern filling his face. He pulled her close and kissed her on the head. "I have no good answer for that, Charlie. Nothing that's going to put you at ease, at least."

Nessie cautiously padded to the stone and sniffed.

"Nessie, here!" Charlie feared something else would fly through the window and strike the dog. Nessie reluctantly left the kitchen and met them in the living room. She sat on Lachlan's feet and leaned hard against his legs. "You know, I was the one who went after her, yet she's showing you all the affection."

"That's because you weren't the one who fed her. Of course I'm going to be her favorite. Plus, I'm the alpha. Clearly."

Charlie rolled her eyes. "Do you have the tools in the house to patch up the board?"

"Yeah, I left them in the pantry. I'll get it taken care of."

Feeling slightly better, Charlie released her death grip and sat on the floor with Nessie while they watched Lachlan get to work. She tried not to stare—too obviously at least—as his back muscles moved under his T-shirt with each whack of the hammer.

"He's going to be the death of me," Charlie whispered in Nessie's ear as she pet the dog.

"What was that?" Lachlan said from the kitchen.

"Nothing. Just talking to Nessie."

He raised an eyebrow and grinned before turning to the window and finishing up. "We're all set. At least for now," he said as he made his way to the living room again. "From what I can see, this storm doesn't seem to be letting up."

Charlie groaned and hugged Nessie closer. "Will this ever end?"

"You two could be twins with your red hair."

She stuck her tongue out at him.

"Careful. Don't stick it out if you don't intend on using it." He winked.

She shook her head in mock disapproval, unable to suppress the smile forming on her lips. Trying to keep things uncomplicated was going to be tough when he was like this. Every sexy remark made her want to say screw it to the ground rules they'd set.

"You're impossible, Lachlan Hart."

The way his eyes gleamed changed her mood from playful to something else. Seeing him like this, so full of life, had gotten under her skin. In those flirty moments, she could see past all the worries she had. Past the man who made her miserable. She found him endearing, sincere, and damn *hot*.

Before she knew what she was doing, she was standing before him. When she bit her bottom lip, all the humor left Lachlan's face, leaving a smoldering look in its wake. His pupils dilated, making his eyes darker and alluring as if they held the secrets to all the pleasures he could make come true for her.

Feeling bold, Charlie lifted to her tiptoes and wrapped her arms around his neck. "And what do you propose I do with this tongue?"

Screw the rules.

Lachlan grabbed her hips, kneading them with strong fingers as he pulled her body flush against his. "I thought we agreed this was complicated." His half argument held no weight as he grazed his lips along her neck.

"Damage has already been done, don't you think? What's the harm in giving in now?" She shrugged a shoulder casually, playing devil's advocate. But she didn't feel casual, not by a long shot.

"You make a valid point." Lachlan ran his tongue along the hollow of her throat, placing a kiss at the bottom.

She let out a ragged breath. Unable to take it anymore, she placed his face between both her hands, pulled his head up, and kissed him. It had the intensity from last night, but now with another layer of hunger. This kiss was not one of restraint or hesitancy, as it was before. Now it was about exploration. Feeling. Primal instinct.

Lachlan trailed his hand up her neck, leaving goose bumps in its wake. Every fiber in her being ached for him to touch her. To take her. To show her he wanted her just as badly as she wanted him.

Needed him.

Three years of emotions—frustration, disappointment, lust, appreciation—all conflicting, all threatening to break her apart if she didn't have some form of release. She looked into his eyes and saw longing reflected there, confirming he felt the same.

They were in this together.

He placed his hand at the base of her head, gripping her hair lightly. He sucked and nipped at her lips, groaning against her mouth as she met him kiss for kiss with feverish passion.

Charlie hopped and circled her legs around his trim waist, wanting every inch of her body against his. Lachlan grabbed her ass to hold her in place and walked across the room, pushing her firmly between the wall and his solid body. As if they had a mind of their own, Lachlan's hips ground against her, and she felt his impressively hard desire right where she wanted him most.

Her clothes were a prison, stopping her from getting the freedom she wanted: Lachlan. Inside her. Making her scream his name over and over. Helping her live out the fantasies that had tortured her since he had arrived on the island.

She rubbed her center against him, eliciting another deep groan from him. He pulled away to give her a good look. His face was flushed from arousal, his eyes wild. He was raw and real, right there for her to see, and it turned her on like nothing else.

Charlie knew she wouldn't stop. She didn't want to. It was as if her life depended on feeling her bare skin against his. He snaked a hand up her shirt, his fingers finding her nipples, and played with them with expert precision. She moaned. Her stomach clenched.

How could something so simple feel so good?

She was lost in the bliss of Lachlan's lips and hands when the sound of the world imploding shook her to the core. He ripped his mouth away and placed her on the floor, shoving her behind his body for protection.

"What is that?" she screamed over the loud noise.

A teeth-chattering *thud* hit the house, and it shook with such force, she thought it would collapse right on top of them. Whirring wind ripped down the staircase, blasting them both with cold, wet air.

"The window again?"

Lachlan gave a tight shake of his head, as if knowing the answer before he confirmed. "No. Stay here."

She reached out to stop him, but he was too fast, making his way up the stairs two at a time. Moments later, he was pulling the mattress down the stairs.

"What the hell are you doing?" She grabbed one end and helped him place the mattress in the living room.

"That loud sound? Part of the roof caved into the master bedroom. It's a mess up there." Without further explanation, he raced back up the stairs, bringing down their belongings, blankets, and pillows in two trips.

Charlie tried to keep it together, but it was hard. Not only was she worried the rest of the roof would cave in, exposing them to the raging storm outside, but also her plan to restore the house was going to become costly if the damage got any worse. She hadn't asked Kennedy if there was insurance on the home.

Another loud crash came from above, startling them both. Charlie's brave face wavered as wind howled from upstairs. Tears filled her eyes, pooling in them and falling over.

Lachlan came to her side, wiping them away with the pads of his thumb. He pulled her to him and rocked her. "Shhh. We'll be okay. I have you, Charlie."

"This house is about to come tumbling down on us. How can you be so certain?"

"Maybe the house won't be standing, but I'm absolutely certain I'll do anything to keep you safe."

She wrapped her arms around his middle and held him tight. His solid, steady body instilled a belief in his words. She would trust him. She had to.

Lachlan let her go to put the sheets and comforter on the mattress, encouraging her to take a seat and relax. "There's nothing more we can do other than wait," he said. "We just have to sit and wait."

Charlie sat, wrapping herself in the heavy blanket for comfort. It was funny that Lachlan was telling them they needed to be patient. For as long as she had known him, they were going a thousand miles a minute. New York was like that, but working at a tech company in New York was a whole beast of its own.

Lachlan settled next to her, and Nessie followed. He held Charlie in his arms and gently rocked her again, like soothing a child who had a night terror. And although Charlie had been on her own for some time, learning to be strong and independent from her mother and Aunt Violet, she welcomed the comfort Lachlan provided. In fact, she melted into it.

"My aunt said this place was magic," she said after some time.

"Hmm?"

"She left a note with her will about this place. She said it was really special, and she hoped I'd find what I was looking for, as she and my uncle had when they first came across it." Another tear rolled down her cheek. "Now it's falling apart."

"Why did you come?" He asked the question softly, likely curious about what caused her to jet-set to Scotland unexpectedly. As far as he knew, it was out of character for her.

"Aside from missing my aunt and wanting to see if this could be a piece of her I could hold on to for years to come?"

Lachlan nodded, sweeping her wild hair away from her face. His eyes were soulful and searching.

"I needed to take a step out of my life to make sure that what I was doing was right. I used to be a different person. I used to be free and curious and hopeful. But then reality hit. Growing up and having to become an adult stripped that from me. I started making decisions based on what was reasonable and expected of me. What was dutiful. What would ensure I could pay my bills. As the years dragged on, a lot of the decisions I made lacked heart. You know? Maybe everyone experiences that." She shrugged it off.

He paused, looking as if she'd struck a chord with him. He let out a breath and shoved a hand through his hair. "More than you know."

"Then you can understand how suffocating that could be. The constant battle between who I should be and who I wanted to be and what I wanted out of life. Every day that passed, working for you," she emphasized, feeling slightly guilty at the wince he gave, "silenced the voice deep within me, begging to make a choice for myself and not because it was right. Changing my career is a huge risk, especially living in New York. What if I can't find a job and run out of savings? What if it turns out to be something I don't actually like? What if I get sucked into another workplace that works me so much I lose the voice again? New York's not an easy place to survive financially.

"I needed a moment. I needed to think through the 'what ifs' and figure out what I'd do if any of those situations actually happened. I had to clear my head, throw myself in a different setting, and just stop all the noise of everyday life so I could hear myself."

"And what did you come to find?"

She bit her bottom lip and stole a quick glance at him. "To be determined. It's kinda hard to hear your inner voice over the sound of whipping wind and a collapsing house." She took his hand and intertwined her fingers with his. "And I had expected to be alone."

"Sorry to have ruined your plans." He kissed the inside of her wrist.

Her skin prickled with goose bumps. "I wouldn't have survived here without you."

"You might not have been stuck here had it not been for me." He gave a guilty, self-deprecating shrug.

"True. But I forgive you. Maybe this isn't the most ideal situation, but it gave me the chance to get to know you. In a way, it's helped me feel less angry about everything." A dry laugh escaped her. "I couldn't wait to get away from you."

"Ouch."

Charlie shot him a look. "Can you blame me?"

"I guess not."

"But now, I'm starting to understand why you pushed so hard. And I'm starting to see there's more to you than I would have thought. I...I like it." More than she wanted to admit.

Lachlan kissed her lightly on the lips, making her stomach do a little flip. "I feel the same. I'm finding so much more about you that I would never have known. What a fool I've been not to take the time to see you and know you."

"It probably wouldn't have been appropriate to know your assistant on this level." She kissed him back, lingering just a bit longer. "Very cliché and likely a legal issue."

He laughed, a sound that gave her a sense of peace and comfort. "You're right, but it doesn't mean I couldn't have made an effort to try to get to know you a little more than as my assistant. Attraction aside, I could have had a real conversation with you."

"We're having it now, at least."

And these days with him posed a new problem for Charlie: how could she ever imagine life without him in it? Each second with him at the cottage solidified that worry, burying itself deep in her soul.

She could fall in love with a guy like Lachlan Hart. As these moments ticked on, she wondered if she had already started to.

CHAPTER NINETEEN

LACHLAN COULD FALL for a woman like Charlie Middleton.

He knew it. Plain and simple. Being around her made him believe he could be different. Better. That maybe the guilt he'd been harboring about Matteo's accident wasn't his to bear.

But would the reality of that belief lay beyond the walls of this *somewhat* safe cottage on the remote Scottish island? Once they got on that ferry—back to civilization—who would he be? The man Charlie made him believe in or the shell of a man he had become these last few years?

Charlie had said her aunt Violet believed this place was magic. In a sense, it was for him. Miraculously, he started to believe in himself again. Trust that he could change his life if he just took the initiative. And if he did decide to move on, that he wouldn't be screwing over his best friend and business partner.

But magic could be fickle. An illusion. All his high hopes could come crashing down on him as soon as the demands of life had him moving at breakneck speed again, never allowing for time to think of this revelation anymore. Or when he saw Matteo struggle to remember something as simple as his son's name. Would the guilt hold him back?

More importantly, did Charlie deserve that? A man who would fall back to his old ways, ones that had her running away as fast as she could?

Charlie had big dreams for herself, and she should achieve every single one of them. Her future was hers for the taking. It would gut him to know he got in the way like he had all those years. What kind of person took away the little inner voice she spoke of?

He shook his head. He couldn't take all the credit. It was life. Becoming an adult was demanding, and they were all prone to making difficult choices. A person couldn't simply follow every single whimsical hope they had.

Could they?

One thing he knew for sure was that talking to Charlie and getting to know her on a deeper level had touched him in ways he couldn't put into words. She was reaching deep down into the recesses of his soul, leaving a lasting mark. Even if he couldn't have her, she'd always be with him.

He hoped he'd leave an impression on her too, one not so easy to forget. Maybe by letting her go and giving up the idea she'd come back as his assistant, he would.

Hours had passed, the two of them side by side on the mattress, looking up at the blank ceiling like it held all the answers to the universe. Maybe it did for them, both lost in their own thoughts. Nessie was curled at their feet, fast asleep. Her paws occasionally twitched like she was running, which made him softly chuckle.

Could life be as simple and as perfect as this?

"I hope you find what you're looking for and go after what makes you happy. And I hope you never doubt it was the right choice. If you do, and it turns out to not be what you wanted, I hope you pivot as soon as you can so you don't get stuck like you've been. You have a lot to offer this world. I'd hate for you to have to wait years to show it just because you're making decisions on what's expected and not what feels right to you."

Lachlan's breath lodged itself in his throat. Had he ever said something so raw? He meant every word, and the emotion in his voice showed it.

She knew it too. She didn't have to look at him. Didn't have to speak. He could tell by the way her breathing steadied and how she grabbed his hand and held tight that what he said mattered to her.

Nothing could touch them here.

"Thank you," she said on a breath.

"I wish I was as brave as you."

She laughed softly at that. "What are you talking about? You've done extraordinary things, Lach."

"My success has gone from doing what I loved, to doing what's right. Like you, that means I've fallen into the same trap that silences my inner voice."

She turned on her side to face him and stroked her delicate hand along his jaw, sending a rush of desire and affection through him. Just that simple gesture.

"I know now that part of the reason you work so hard is because of the guilt you have about Matteo. But it was an accident, Lachlan. It wasn't your fault. You have to let that go."

"You're right. Maybe it's time for me to move on from MindThrive AI too." It was shocking, even to his own ears. But the admission came from somewhere deep inside his core, a place he'd snuffed out with his drive and ambition.

Charlie gasped, her going eyes wide. "Move on? It's everything to you."

He gave a tight smile. "It's something to me. Not everything. There has to be more to life than focusing only on one area." His smile turned more genuine. "Or at least that's what my mother tells me. But I think she says it to trick me into giving her grandkids so I'll visit more often."

Charlie giggled. "Maybe so, but I think she's right. I want a well-rounded life. Something filled with more than responsibilities and expectations. If I'm going to have expectations, I want it to be ones I set for myself, not what I think others want from me."

There was a tightness in his chest as another insightful tidbit from Charlie struck home, finally putting into words the unsettled feeling that had coursed through him for years. He thought the feeling was because he was missing some key elements in life, such as hobbies, friends, or a lover. He didn't realize part of the issue had to do with the expectations placed on him. Matteo had never asked him to take on the brunt of the work, but Lachlan felt he had to.

Lachlan Hart: tech genius, business-savvy, and a hell of a business partner. The summation had backed him into a corner. *He* had backed himself into a corner.

Could he break away from those expectations, or was it too late? If so, what would be next?

As soon as the question popped in his head, so did the answer.

His grammar school had reached out to him, looking for him to come in and get kids excited about STEM. Hadn't that been the whole reason he'd gotten into tech to begin with? Yes, he had always liked to dabble. Loved pulling things apart and figuring it out. But it wasn't until a guest speaker—one of the other student's parents—had come in to talk about computer science that he had considered it.

The speaker painted such a wonderful picture, showing Lachlan he could push boundaries as far as he wanted to. If something didn't exist, he could invent it. He could change the world, no matter how minor his invention was.

So he did.

Although the world had become more tech-savvy in the years since he'd grown up, with new discoveries that were beyond his imagination even in college, the shortage of STEM talent was still horrendous. Part of the issue was educating kids at a young age about what they could do and what a career in tech could be. The other part was giving them the tools and knowledge to build necessary skills.

It was even worse for under-resourced communities. There was so much untapped talent just because they lived in the wrong place and didn't have the mentors.

But he could be a mentor. He could be the difference.

He could instill passion in these impressionable minds as he had done to him all those years ago. And maybe, through this, he'd find *his* passion again. His purpose.

"I think I'm going to start an incubator." He said the words slowly, getting a feel for them. Unsure yet inspired.

Charlie raised her eyebrows. "What do you mean?"

"To give back to the community. To make a new generation of Lachlan Harts."

She rolled her eyes but grinned. "Ego much?"

"And Lachlaney Harts. Can't forget to support women in STEM."

She shook her head, a smile still on her lips. "And how do you propose that? What's this 'incubator?'"

"Not sure yet. Maybe it will be a new curriculum for grammar and high school students. Maybe it will be an after-school program. All I know is that it will be free for students."

"Free?" She didn't hide her surprise.

"And maybe I'll find a way to offer transportation for those in rougher areas so they all have an opportunity to attend. I'll work to lower the barrier to entry."

Charlie looked at him, half astounded and half admiring. She didn't speak for some time, simply stroked his face with a gentle hand.

"I think it's a wonderful idea," she finally said. "Do you think MindThrive is going to let you go so easily?"

Lachlan lifted a shoulder. "I'm not sure. But it's worth doing whatever I can to leave the company in good hands if I decide to really pursue this." He turned on his side to face her and kissed her slowly. Tenderly. "This is all because of you," he whispered against her lips.

"Me?"

"You made me see I wasn't in control of my life as much as I believed. And now, I have the opportunity to do something about it. It just feels right, like maybe the idea had been inside me all along, waiting to make itself known when I was ready to acknowledge it."

"I don't think I can take all the credit for that." She bit his bottom lip playfully, making him groan.

"You're an amazing woman, Charlie. There's no one else in the world I would rather be stranded on an island with than you. You make me better. You always have. But now it's so much more. More than I could have ever thought." His voice shook. "I can't picture my life without you in it. I don't want to."

"So don't," she said breathlessly before kissing him again.

CHAPTER TWENTY

CHARLIE WANTED Lachlan more than she had ever wanted anything. Right now. Here. In the midst of a storm, on a deserted island, in front of a fireplace in an otherwise crumbling house.

It was almost laughable. A wealthy tech guru who was always surrounded by beauty, innovation, and a flock of people desperate for his approval seemed the most attractive here.

His clean-shaven face had grown thick, dark scruff. His clothes were a simple T-shirt and jeans. And he was constantly pushing his hair off his forehead. It was a stark contrast from the man who was always dashing and polished. The man that women would fall over for.

Yet somehow, here, he seemed the most comfortable. Most happy. And inspired again, if his revelation was any indication. He amazed her.

And she wanted him. Just like this.

There would be no stopping this time. The whole house could come down on them, and it couldn't keep her from having him.

Her heart banged against her ribs as the light from the fireplace flickered in his eyes, reflecting the fire burning deep inside her belly.

"I want this. I want you."

"Are you sure?" His voice was low, rumbling his chest against hers.

"Yes."

"This will change everything between us." The statement had a certain restraint to it, as if he were trying to do the noble thing but also was praying she wouldn't change her mind.

"It already has, Lach."

That was all he needed. He flipped Charlie onto her back, disrupting Nessie's nap, and causing the dog to scurry away to the kitchen where she could sleep in peace.

Lachlan kneeled on the mattress and hovered over her, making him larger than life. The wind and rain battering the house faded away when she looked up at him, and found longing and desire in his expression. To know he felt that way about her, that *she* was the one making him feel that way, did things to her.

She reached for him, her body aching to feel him. Gripping the hem of his T-shirt, she pulled it over his head, revealing the perfectly sculpted body underneath, complete with the tattoo on his shoulder —a tribute to his former life. Or maybe a life he was about to rediscover. The light from the fire glowed across his skin, creating dark shadows that defined the valleys of his muscles.

Muscles she wanted pressed against her body. Now.

Kneeling up to meet him, she ran her hands over his body freely as she caught his lips again in a deep, seductive kiss. Lachlan snaked his fingers under the bottom of her shirt, and he let out a long, shuddering breath as he trailed his fingers along her back. She savored the feel of his rough fingertips tracing her smooth skin and nearly lost her mind when he pushed the cup of her bra aside to circle her nipple with his thumb. They budded instantly, aching to be pinched and licked.

Desperate for more, Charlie hastily pulled her shirt off. Lachlan stilled, his gaze wandering over every curve of her body. He reached behind her, unhooked her bra, and pulled it slowly down her arms and away from her body, appreciating the view of every exposed inch.

Bending his head, he took one of her nipples into his mouth, the warmth against her skin driving her insane.

The air was charged, and as he ran his hands along her body, she knew this moment mattered. She let go of any lingering reservations or worries, finally feeling safe to give herself fully to him.

She lost herself as he took his time between licking and gently nibbling. When she couldn't take it anymore, she pulled him up to kiss her and pressed her body against his. Bare skin against bare skin felt explosive, and they'd barely gotten started. How Lachlan could stay steady, taking his time to enjoy every moment, was beyond her.

Every muscle in her body tensed, waiting for sweet relief. Charlie needed him. She was a desperate woman, and only he could be the one that gave her the release.

Her breathing grew ragged and harsh as she moved her shaky hands to the button of his jeans and unbuttoned them. Her insides fluttered. Letting her guard down was unnerving, but she wanted it to be *him*. She wanted Lachlan to be the one to gain access to her now that her walls were down.

And she wanted to trust he'd take care of her *and* her heart.

She pulled down the zipper and slid her hand inside to feel his solid length, pulling him free. She broke the kiss just enough to look down, tormented by the vision of her delicate hand wrapped around his rock-hard cock. She was momentarily mesmerized by its beauty and power.

It was all for her.

Lachlan sucked in a breath as she stroked her hand up and down. He squeezed his eyes shut and gritted his teeth. "You're killing me."

She gave him another solid stroke, rubbing her hand over the head and spreading its moisture around.

He let out a mix of a growl and a groan.

"Just returning the favor," she said in a sultry tone.

Seeing his response to her touch made her feel powerful. Desired. If the overwhelming need to have him inside her that instant wasn't a factor, she might have teased him more just to see him come apart.

For as long as she'd known Lachlan, he'd always been so perfect. So put together. But seeing his raw reaction made it seem like she was in on some sexy secret. One that only she would know.

That maybe this side of him was only reserved for her eyes.

Charlie used her free hand to unbutton her pants and took his hand, guiding it in between her legs, allowing him to dip his finger inside her so he could see she was equally turned on, if not more. Lachlan let out another shuddering breath as he pressed into her, taking control and feeling her warm wetness sliding on his finger.

Whatever little restraint Lachlan was holding on to at that moment disappeared. Before she knew it, he had her on her back with her jeans pulled off and tossed across the room. He was a man on a mission, eager to explore and taste the splendors of her body. She was more than happy to oblige.

Lachlan hovered over her, using his thumb to rub the sensitive nub between her legs as he kissed his way down from her mouth, neck, breasts, and stomach. She arched her back, feeling the pleasure build in her with each circle of his finger. He was a pro, knowing exactly how to touch her with just the right pressure and rhythm. It was as if his hands were made to please her, that his whole life was dedicated to doing only that. The warmth of his mouth traveled lower past her navel, then he pulled her panties down her legs and threw them to the side with her discarded jeans.

As soon as she was free from her clothing, Lachlan was back on her, kissing her deliciously slow on her inner thighs, coming closer and closer to where his fingers were working their magic.

The instant his tongue was on her, she thought she would explode. Her hips bucked, but Lachlan held them in place, forcing her to experience every single sensation of his tongue. He stuck two fingers inside her to gauge her pleasure, stroking her from the inside as he licked her bundle of nerves. She tightened around him, ready to climax. Only a couple more strokes of his tongue, and she'd be over the edge.

She moaned his name, the sound of it echoing against the empty walls, as he licked her into oblivion. Her legs—resting over his shoulders—shook wildly with each thunderous pulse from her orgasm. Her skin flushed and stomach clenched as he lapped at her, letting her ride out her orgasm for as long as her body would allow.

When it finally subsided into tiny, weak pulsations, she went limp like a rag doll. Her bones had melted away. She grabbed his wrist as he tried to shift to her side. "Where do you think you're going?"

Lachlan lifted her other arm and watched it flop onto the bed. "Just letting you recover." A satisfied grin filled his face.

Charlie rolled to face him. "Although that was probably the most amazing thing I ever felt—"

"Probably?"

"Okay. It *was* the most amazing thing I've ever felt. I want to do that again. But this time, I want you inside me. All of you. Every inch," she said between her heaving breaths.

He raised an eyebrow. "Is that so?" Although he was trying to play coy, Charlie caught his cock twitch out of the corner of her eye.

She reached out to slide his pants off completely. Pulling him on top of her, she felt his hardness press against her stomach. "Tell me you want me too." She was desperate to hear the words fall from his lips.

All joking had left Lachlan's face. "More than anything." He paused. "I don't have a condom."

"I'm on the pill, and I'm clean. You?"

He nodded. "Are you sure you want this?"

As a response, Charlie reached down, positioning him in between the junction of her thighs. He hissed out a breath when the tip of his cock connected with her wetness. She bit her bottom lip and raised her heels to push into his ass, urging him to fill her up.

Through clenched teeth, Lachlan moved into her with care, allowing her body to adjust to him. Inch by inch, thrust by thrust, he drove a little deeper. When he finally made it to the hilt, both of them moaned.

Nothing had ever felt as good as this.

Lachlan lowered himself, wrapping his arms underneath her head for support, and kissed her deeply as he pushed into her again. The rhythm was still slow, and she thought she would die from the bliss, loving how he filled her up.

He wanted to make it last. And for Charlie, as much as she wanted him, she was perfectly fine with it. She loved how he drove into her over and over, the way the friction built between them.

How close he was to her, their bodies only illuminated by the warm glow of the fireplace. It might have been the most intimate moment she'd ever experienced.

She gripped his back, her hands slipping on the slick sweat from the exertion. Breaking the kiss, she caught his gaze. His face was full of lust, his eyes hooded, as he concentrated on the motion of his body with hers. He was lost in it. Lost in her. He looked at her and smiled.

Lachlan slipped a hand from under her head and reached between them, finding her sensitive spot again and stroking it in circles. He picked up the tempo as he ground his hips into her faster.

He watched her with voyeuristic interest as she came close to the brink of another orgasm. "Come for me, Charlie," he whispered roughly in her ear as he moved his fingers in tight, quick circles.

Those words pushed her over the edge. She dug her nails into his back as she lifted her hips to take more of him. Shock waves of pleasure rushed through her, knocking the wind out of her as her body clench around him. Coming while wrapped around him only amplified it. Lachlan let out a guttural groan and gave into his own pleasure, riding it out with several more thrusts.

Afterward, he collapsed on top of her in a sated heap. The feel of her slick skin against his was addicting. She pushed the hair away from his forehead and looked into his cerulean-blue eyes, now half open as he came down from the rush.

He buried his face in her neck and rolled to the side, pulling her with him. Their legs stayed twisted together as they caught their breath.

"I think I've found my new obsession," he said against her neck.

"If you're referring to what we just did, I'd happily accept being your vice." She kissed his shoulder and gave it a light bite.

Within moments, they fell asleep. Still naked and tangled together. It was the best sleep Charlie probably ever had.

* * *

"Charlie," a voice whispered, followed by a hand pushing her hair away from her face.

She opened her eyes to find Lachlan hovering over her. "What's going on?" Her voice was thick with sleep.

"The storm. I think it's nearly over."

She shifted and listened. The wind and rain that had relentlessly pelted the cottage was nonexistent. "What time is it?"

"Just after four in the morning."

After a brief nap earlier, Lachlan and Charlie had woken up for another round, that time slower and more intimate. And then another round again a few hours after that. Her body felt sore in all the best ways, a reminder he had been inside her. A reminder that made her want to push him down on the bed, get on top of him, and let him fill her up again.

Would she ever get enough of him? Would these feelings ever stop surprising her? Lachlan was the last person on earth who she'd thought would ever bring out this side of her. And now, he was all she wanted. She *craved* him.

"Judging by that faraway look on your face, I have a feeling you're thinking of round four." He smiled. "As much as I would love that, maybe we should see what's going on?"

She scowled, hating his voice of reason. She wrapped the comforter around her naked body and made her way to the back door, pulling it open cautiously as if the terrible storm was waiting outside to pounce on her just when she thought it was safe. But when she opened it, there was no sinister storm lurking there. Through the darkness of early morning, she could make out the stars in the sky. Not a single drop of rain fell. Aside from a gentle breeze, the wind had disappeared.

They had made it through the storm.

CHAPTER TWENTY-ONE

VENTURING OUTSIDE CAUTIOUSLY, they took in the sights around them. Nessie bounded ahead, thrilled to be able to go out and pop a squat. As Charlie led them to the front of the house, she got a good look at what she'd have to add to her growing punch list. Standing by the front gate—or what was left of it—she sucked in a breath. Like a beacon of resilience in the dim morning light, the cottage still stood, for the most part, but it had taken one hell of a beating.

Most of the windows upstairs were shattered. A few stones had come loose and fallen from the exterior of the house and the stone fence. Part of the roof had caved in. Trees and bushes were uprooted.

She buried her face in her hands. How was she going to afford to fix all of this on top of the other repairs? The cottage would need a complete overhaul. Despite the harrowing events from these last few days, Charlie was convinced she needed to do whatever she could to keep this place, even if it meant going broke trying. She had fallen in love with it.

How could she ever let it go? But how could she afford to keep it?

Lachlan whistled, and Nessie came barreling back to them. That poor dog was probably antsy after being trapped in the house.

Thankfully, she seemed to be in much better spirits than when Charlie had originally found her. She only hoped Callum, the grocer, would be back soon to get her.

Lachlan's warm, strong hand enveloped hers. "Come on. Let's see what we're working with here."

They left the property and walked to an area down the street that provided a good lookout to the main road. The water had started to recede but had left disaster in its wake. The pavement had cracked and come up in areas. Debris and sand from the sea littered the roads. Some buildings had taken a similar beating as her cottage had, and she wondered how bad the water damage was. Luckily, her house was just high enough to stay out of the storm surge, but the area below wasn't as lucky.

At least the dock still stood strong, if not a bit battered with its missing wood planks. But as long as it was there, that meant the boats could come back to get them.

Charlie's body felt heavy as she looked to the bleak scene in front of her. "This is horrible." Boats and cars were piled up in soaked heaps. The lush trees along the streets were leveled, snagging power lines on their way down.

"Reminds me of Hurricane Sandy. My hometown was in shambles." Lachlan looked down at her. "Don't you remember?"

"I flew to Savannah to be with my mom and worked remotely until things were back in working order." She exhaled. "My mom must be so worried. I told her I'd check in with her every day. I haven't talked to her since I first got to the island."

Lachlan peered out to the horizon. "It looks like the water isn't churning as much. Might mean help will be on the way soon."

"I hope so."

They stood there for some time, watching the whitecaps of the ocean become sparser and the thick gray clouds float away like a distant memory. Blue skies peeked out, offering a reprieve from a dark and dreary day. As a beam of light pushed through a break in the clouds, lighting up what once was a beautiful main street of the tiny island village, Charlie felt a sense of peace and purpose.

Maybe the Isle of Murdina would never be the same. Maybe it would take some time for it to repair itself. And maybe it would take her a while to save money needed to fix the cottage her late aunt had left her. But she would do it. She would rebuild, like the rest of the Scottish islanders. Maybe she'd luck out and learn the cottage had insurance. That could help.

She'd find a way.

She'd go back home and do her bootcamp as she'd planned. She wouldn't accept any job offers that had a base salary less than needed to save for repairs or wouldn't offer enough flexibility to allow her to come here regularly.

Lachlan squeezed her hand, breaking her thoughts. "You have that determined look on your face. What's going on?"

"Trying to figure out what I can do to save my aunt's house. *My* house."

He nodded. "It's going to get pretty pricey." He turned to face her, taking both of her hands in his. "I can help."

Charlie's eyebrows knitted in confusion. "What do you mean?"

"Let me pay for the repairs. It clearly means the world to you, and I want to support you as you've done for me through the years."

Charlie froze, and her stomach dropped. Lachlan's face was so hopeful, so reassuring. He was confident he could snap his fingers and fix all her problems without a second thought. Maybe he could with the type of money he'd earned over the years. But that wasn't how Charlie did things, nor was it her reality. If anything, his suggestion only reminded her of how grossly different their lives were.

He had the world at his fingertips, and she needed to work hard to earn her place in the world. She refused to take handouts.

She bristled when she realized he hadn't even made it off the island, yet he was already reverting to his old self. If there was a roadblock, fix it swiftly. Throw money at it. Make it go away so he could forge on.

Her rose-colored glasses shattered, filtering in his true colors through the cracks.

"Thanks. But no." Her voice was icier than she meant it to be.

Lachlan's face dropped. "What?"

"I've got this."

Realization crossed his face. She was putting up walls, and she knew he knew it.

"The cottage is important to you," he started, attempting a different approach. "I just wanted to offer to help. It's going to be a huge undertaking."

"I may not be a millionaire, but I think I can understand the basics of home repair costs."

"What's gotten into you?" His body went rigid, and his eyebrows furrowed.

He was confused, and she couldn't blame him. She had gone from hot to cold in an instant. She owed him an explanation, but couldn't find the words. Not now while her head and heart were battling it out. She had started to fall for the man she discovered in the quiet confines of the cottage. He'd given her false hope that he truly could be that man.

I'm such a fool.

Logic came rushing back, reminding her that people didn't change overnight. His simple offer to help proved that. He would always be Lachlan Hart.

It would be best to get rid of any delusions that they could be something—that he could be different with her—before she got any deeper.

CHAPTER TWENTY-TWO

IT DIDN'T TAKE A GENIUS—THE media's word, not his—to know something had changed with Charlie. Her hand felt limp in his when Lachlan guided them back to the cottage to wait for the rescue crew. It was almost laughable how she tried to casually push hair from her face, giving her the excuse to pull away from him.

But it wasn't the lack of PDA that struck him as odd. No. It was the fact that the hopeful glint that brightened her big green eyes had vanished and was replaced with lackluster dullness. He wanted to believe she was just overwhelmed with the idea of house repairs, but he knew that wasn't it. Not with the invisible dome she had strategically placed around herself keep him at a distance. Somehow, they'd reverted to how it was when he first arrived.

What happened to the woman who was so hungry with lust that she couldn't keep her hands off him? What happened to the person who bared her soul to him?

Somehow, he felt even more disconnected from her than he had in the years he'd known her. He was untethered, as if he were about to spiral out of control, lost forever. He was desperate to regain their connection. Charlie had helped him make sense of his world. Had shown him there was more to life. And after being trapped on this island with her, he couldn't fathom her not being in his.

Lachlan opened the door of the cottage. Charlie dipped under his arm and trudged through the house, her footsteps heavy on the wooden floors. Nessie scurried in after her.

He sighed, hating how distant she was being. "Charlie. What's going on?"

She grabbed a log and busied herself with tending to the fire, purposely avoiding his gaze. He could see the tension in her shoulders as they lifted to her ears. "Nothing."

"Clearly—" Lachlan was cut short by the ringing of a cell phone.

Charlie shot him a look, her eyes narrowing, almost daring him.

To do what?

The phone stopped ringing, but now incessant pings for emails and text messages blared through the house.

Standing, Charlie crossed her arms. "You gonna get that?" She raised an eyebrow. "Seems like the world can't wait to hear from you."

Yup. There's that Ice Queen again.

Lachlan shoved a hand through his hair and debated on how to approach this situation, but the constant buzz from his cell phone grated on his nerves, distracting him from any coherent thoughts. He held up a finger. "One second."

She gave a passive-aggressive shrug and rolled her eyes before sitting on the floor to pet Nessie.

Lachlan went to the kitchen, finding his phone on the counter where he had left it charging before the electricity had gone out. He clicked the button to silence the ringer and watched as missed voice mails, texts, and emails piled up. Angry business partners wondered why he bailed on the meeting with the investors. Frustrated investors threatened not to reschedule. Messages from colleagues who were oblivious as to why he wasn't responsive. A few SOSs from the new assistant. Worried texts from Devonny asking if he'd found Charlie.

Hundreds of messages. All urgent.

The tension headache behind his eyes came back almost instantly.

No wonder he found clarity while he was stranded here. He didn't have a damn tension headache melting his brain.

Lachlan's hand hovered over the phone. He had to make a choice: ignore the messages a little bit longer and figure out what was going on with Charlie, or put out the fires and ensure his company's reputation was still intact.

Before he could make the decision, his phone rang with a call from the investors.

"Lachlan Hart," he answered, already hating how phony he sounded. Hating how his subconscious reaction automatically chose business over people. Over her.

Again.

"Lachlan, this is David Wells from Watts and Associates." David's voice was clipped, as if patiently waiting to figure out if he should tell Lachlan to fuck off.

"Mr. Wells. I'm glad you called. I apologize for the missed meeting. I took an unexpected trip and, unfortunately, got stuck in a storm with no ability to communicate that to you or my partners. I had every intention of being there."

"Quite an excuse."

"I'll assure you that I've tried to contact you and my colleagues about the travel issue, but the storm knocked out cell service. It's almost a miracle I have any with the destruction of the island." Of course, his expensive global cell plan would work *after* he needed it.

"To say we were disappointed is an understatement. My associates and I have a lot of people vying for our time and our investments."

"I understand, sir. You've known me for some time now. You know this is very unlike me. It was an unusual circumstance." Lachlan shook his head, pissed at himself for not trusting his colleagues enough to give the presentation in his absence. Had he not been a control freak and believed in his team more, this conversation wouldn't be happening.

And he could focus on Charlie to understand why she was pushing him away, especially after the night they'd just shared. They'd had a breakthrough. He wasn't ready to let it slip through his fingers so soon.

"Yes, Lachlan. We have built a good rapport, which is why I'm calling. I want to reschedule. I believe in what you're doing at MindThrive AI."

"I would appreciate that."

"I'm not saying it's going to be easy convincing the rest of the associates to consider the investment. They're going to be harder to crack after the no-show."

"I understand. I'll do my best to prove their investment is safe."

"All right. I'll have my assistant coordinate with yours on a new date and time."

"That would be great. Thank you."

Lachlan hung up the phone and scrubbed a hand down his face. He should be ecstatic that his trip didn't royally fuck up the chance with the investors. But the relief never came.

"Was that the investment firm?"

Charlie's voice made him jump. He turned to her and leaned his hip against the counter. "Yes. They want to reschedule."

"I'm happy for you."

Then why did she sound so heartbroken about it?

She held up her cell. "My service still isn't working. Can I use yours to call my mom?"

"Sure." Lachlan tossed her the phone. "You might want to check in with Devonny too. I had a few messages from her. She's worried."

She gave a tight nod and disappeared into the living room.

Lachlan faced the counter and placed his hands firmly on the tiled top. Why did it feel like his lungs were about to collapse? His chest constricted, making it difficult to breathe, something he only experienced when he pushed himself hard at the gym.

He was suffocating.

Pushing off the counter, he walked to where Charlie was sitting, trying his hardest to not let the lack of air prevent him from fixing things with her. He needed her presence to make him feel right. Even if she was giving him the cold shoulder, being around her would relieve the heaviness in his chest.

"I love you too, Mama," she murmured before she hung up the phone.

Lachlan took a seat and could feel his chest open again just by being near her. He gave Nessie a good scratch behind the ears. "Everything okay with your mom?"

"She was worried sick, as I expected. When she hadn't heard from me, she called the property manager. Needless to say, they were both anxious when they realized I hadn't gotten off the island." Tears filled her eyes. "I feel so horrible. She must have been scared to death thinking something happened to me, especially right after losing Aunt Violet."

Lachlan took her hand. When he felt her squeeze it for a second, he believed they might be all right.

"Hey," he said softly. "You're okay. You'll be back to see her before you know it."

Charlie pulled her hand away to wipe her eyes. Lachlan tried not to feel crushed when she didn't reach for him again. "I know." She passed him the phone. "I texted Devonny and let her know we're okay."

"Charlie—"

"Someone should be coming soon." She deliberately cut him off, likely to avoid hearing whatever he had to say. "Mom said once Kennedy realized I never came back, he'd promised to get a rescue crew out here as soon as the waters were safe."

Lachlan thought back to the settling sea. "That should be soon."

"Yeah," she said, her voice quiet and sad. She stood. "We better pack."

"Can't you just sit with me? For a moment longer?" His voice was desperate.

Her red-rimmed eyes were full of despair. She opened her mouth to say something, but clamped it shut instead.

He rose and took her shoulders in his hands. Bending slightly, he looked her straight in the eyes. "Tell me what's going on. What happened? Why are you so distant?" When she wouldn't meet his eyes, he urged, "Damn it. Look at me."

Charlie's gaze shot up to his, sadness now replaced with a defiant glint. "What do you want me to say, Lachlan?"

"Why the sudden change? You were fine an hour ago."

She shook off his hands and paced the room. "What were we thinking, Lach? We were in some stupid fantasy here."

He recoiled as if she'd slapped him. "What the hell do you mean?"

She pointed between them. "You and me. How unrealistic is that?"

Anger boiled Lachlan's blood. "We're *not* unrealistic," he said through clenched teeth. "What happened between us is not some fantasy. It was real. It still can be real if you stop finding excuses for why it can't be."

Charlie gave a humorless laugh and threw her hands in the air. "I'm not finding excuses. The truth's in plain sight. The real world crept in the moment the storm was over, and you're already back to who you were in New York." She ran a hand through her hair, a rough motion. "God, I'm such an idiot to think you could be different."

"I am. And I can be," Lachlan grounded out. He crossed the room and took her in his arms, crushing her against his chest. She tried to squirm against him but gave up. "How could you honestly think otherwise?" he whispered.

"You were ready to throw money at the cottage without even a flinch. And the phone call with the investors. I thought you were moving on from MindThrive."

"I was offering to help you because I *care* about you, Charlie. I know how important this cottage is to you, and I don't want you to worry about letting it go. Why can't you see that?"

"If you care about me, then you'd know I prefer to do things on my own. My mom raised me not to depend on anyone."

"I'm sorry if you perceived my offer as a hit to your independence. That wasn't my intention." He could understand her need for independence, but why couldn't she see he was trying to be a support system for her? To give back to her after years of underappreciating her. It was the least he could do.

She deserved so much more.

"And the investors?"

"I can't just up and quit the second I decide I'm ready for something new." He tried to keep his tone steady, but her unrealistic outrage put him on edge. "You know how important it is for me to protect and take care of the employees and Matteo. I need to leave them in good hands. That will take some time. I can't change and immediately drop everything like..."

"Like me," Charlie finished for him. She pushed away. "Who are you without MindThrive, Lachlan? Do you even know?"

"I have an idea, but I won't know until I try."

"I'll tell you what I know about you: you're loyal, ambitious, determined, and you think big. To a fault. I can almost guarantee you'll get back to New York with the grand intentions of moving on from the company, but you'll get sucked right back in. There will always be people who need you there. Always be new pressures and challenges to overcome. And there will always be something that threatens the future of the company. You see things through. It's going to be hard for you to give it up. You won't change."

"I *have* changed. I feel it in the deepest parts of me. Being here, with you, made it that way."

"People can't change in a matter of days, Lachlan. That's not possible. You'll see that once you get back to New York." A single tear fell from her eye. "I wish it was different. I almost believed it was. But it was stupid."

Lachlan pinched his nose, attempting to contain his frustration. He loved her stubbornness, but not when it was used against him. "Why can't people change that fast, Charlie? Huh? You can take your time and make some grand plan for yourself with your milestones and timelines, but life happens. It's messy, exciting, scary, and eye-opening. It can completely derail your best-laid plans. I never planned for the algorithm Matteo and I developed to take off all those years ago. I never planned to take over a whole company when Matteo had his accident. But I embraced it. And you know what I learned when I was thrown into those situations?"

She eyed him suspiciously. "What?"

"When to take a chance, and how to pivot and adapt when you do."

"This isn't some business deal. This is about us and my feelings for you. Being with me isn't going to be cut-and-dried. You can't sign on the dotted line and feel confident you know what you're getting."

"It doesn't matter. I want you, Charlie."

Her features softened a fraction before her defenses went up again. "How would that work? I only know you as my boss. The workaholic. The guy who keeps everyone at arm's length—"

Lachlan's nostrils flared. "Was I that man these last few days?"

"No, but look how quickly you fell back into that role once your cell phone worked. How long can you be the guy trapped in a cottage when you're battling who you were in New York? And once you move on from MindThrive AI, it's going to be hard to figure out who you are again. How do I fit into all of this? How will this be fair to what our relationship could be? Will I fall into the assistant role again except with the illusion that I'm your girlfriend?"

"God. No, Charlie. It won't be like that. I won't let it. I know you're scared, but I need you to trust me. Trust *this*."

Tears filled her eyes. "How do you know? People fall into patterns that feel most familiar. Most comfortable. I don't know you any other way, Lachlan. My life got so entwined with yours that I couldn't find myself. I didn't have a second to put *me* first when I was so busy putting *you* before myself. I can't fall back into that. I can't even chance it," she said frantically. "Somehow, our dynamic will revert back to what it was these last three years. I just know it. We have too much history for it not to. I can't tangle my life with yours again. I can't risk a future I'm set on for a present with you that I'm not sure about."

Her words gutted him, and that untethered feeling intensified.

I'm losing her.

Out of desperation, he reached for her and cupped her face, crushing her lips with his, putting every ounce of feeling behind it. If words couldn't show it, maybe action would.

Lachlan pulled away and looked into her stunned eyes. "I want to be tangled up with you, Charlie. I can't imagine my life without you. I promise you it won't be that way. We can be different."

Charlie leaned into him and wrapped her arms tight around his neck. She pressed her lips against his again, slowly at first, the passion increasing with hunger and emotion. His mouth moved with hers, her plush lips both soft and demanding. He could feel the tears streaming from her eyes on his cheeks, the salty taste of them melding with their kiss.

She pulled away as if coming to her senses, looking absolutely shattered. "You can't possibly know that. You can't promise me that. I'm sorry. I can't, Lachlan."

And just like that, Lachlan realized she had kissed him good-bye.

CHAPTER TWENTY-THREE

SLEEP WAS IMPOSSIBLE THAT NIGHT. To lie next to Lachlan and not reach for him nearly killed Charlie. She could feel the warmth from his body only mere inches from her, and in his sleep, he would pull her close. On more than one occasion, Charlie allowed herself to be held. To do whatever she could to keep this memory because once they left the island, it would be all she had left of him. But whenever she found herself considering the possibilities of giving them a real shot, she pulled herself from his arms and rolled back to her side of the bed.

Cold, lonely, and heartbroken.

How could a matter of days have changed so much for her? How she felt about him? Lachlan touched the deepest parts of her, making her feel alive and cared for in ways she didn't think possible.

Especially not with him.

But he'd proved her wrong. He had shown her there was more to him than she'd initially believed, and she'd liked it. She had *more* than liked it.

Lachlan was convinced they could work. He vowed his commitment to change his ways. She wanted to believe it. Every fiber in her being told her to trust him. But after years of watching her mother try to get through to her grandparents and the constant rejection, Charlie knew people were who they were. No amount of love or big life moments could change who someone innately was.

If her mother's own flesh and blood couldn't change through the years, how could days change the dynamic between her and Lachlan?

Charlie had worked too hard to get to this point in her life. She needed to protect herself, although she knew Lachlan was right when he said he couldn't drop everything in an instant and that he needed time to set things right. She couldn't fault him for it. After all, she knew how much guilt and pressure he had put on himself concerning the company, its people, and Matteo. That level of guilt would be hard to unlearn and let go of. But could she chance it? What if she gave in and lost herself again, only to find that Lachlan couldn't change?

It was easy to say he was going to do something, but the truth was in his actions. She'd believe it when she saw it.

There was too much at risk. When it came to following her heart, she was choosing her career over him. She couldn't do both. It wasn't fair to not give her all to either. At least her career was the safer of the two.

Doesn't that make you a hypocrite? You damned him for choosing his career, and now you're doing the same.

She placed her hand over her mouth to silence the anguish threatening to escape as her tears flowed.

You can't have it all.

Her stomach clenched, and her insides tensed and ached. For hours, her heart and mind were at odds. She accepted that her feelings ran deep for him. Here on this island, how could she not care for the man she'd discovered?

But sometimes love—*lust?*—was short-lived. Just like how her father had been stripped from her mother before they had a chance to become a family, Lachlan would go to New York and fall back into the life he was accustomed to, a life that had no room for anyone else.

It was best if she started fresh with someone else, someone who would fit better in her life. She and Lachlan had far too much history to overcome. Even if he continued on the path he had started here, she would always fear he'd realize he'd made a mistake and eventually slip away from her.

What kind of relationship would that be? Her insecurity would put a strain on them. She'd never be able to give her all to him because of it, and he would resent her for not having enough faith in him.

It would end in a disaster. She just knew it.

He reached for her again and gripped her hips, turning her to face him. She was startled to find his beautiful blue eyes open. He wasn't reaching for her in a sleep-induced haze. He wanted her.

"Charlie." His voice was hoarse from sleep. "Please." The simple word held the weight of the world. He was begging for her to reconsider. To believe in him. To not let go.

But she couldn't, and that was on her. The pain she was causing both of them was all her fault, but it was for the best.

Maybe one day she'd believe that.

She lifted a shaky hand and stroked his cheek, trying to memorize his face, so full of tortured hope. His eyes, now glassy and red, searched for any indication she would change her mind.

He placed a hand over hers, careful not to hurt her healing wound. "I can't do this without you. I don't want to." He swallowed hard. "Please."

Charlie's throat constricted, and she was thankful for it. It prevented her from saying the words that were threatening to come out.

I want to be with you. Please mean what you say. My heart is cracking in two at the thought of letting you go.

Don't let me let you go.

She breathed in deep, battling with what she wanted versus what should be. His earnest pleading made it near impossible for her to stay strong.

A horn sounded, pulling them from their quiet, intimate moment. Breaking their safe haven.

The real world was closing in.

They both listened. Another long, throaty bellow came a few seconds later.

Lachlan looked at her, his eyes pained once again. "Rescue crews. They're here."

They had prayed to get off this island alive, but now that the reality of it was here, Charlie was overwhelmed. The sound of the rescue crews coming meant this really was over. And soon, Lachlan would be on his way to the mainland and back to America while she stayed behind to pick up the pieces.

Of the cottage. Of her heart.

They got up and reluctantly gathered their things. Charlie stayed silent so her voice wouldn't betray her. She caught a glance of Lachlan from the corner of her eye as his shoulders sagged in defeat. For a man who was a bulldozer in business, he gave up on Charlie so easily.

It's for the best.

Moments later, someone pounded on the door. "Is anyone in there?" a deep voice boomed from the other side.

Lachlan gripped the door handle and looked at Charlie. One last look before he let the real world back in.

Her mouth dropped open, wanting to beg him to wait a moment longer. Just to hold on to one more minute with him and the dream that they could work. But the door pushed open before she could utter a word.

Everything moved in slow motion as shock, heartache, and relief washed over Charlie. A group of first responders flooded the house, taking them outside to check for injuries and trauma. The crew tended to Charlie's foot and hand and wrapped Lachlan and Charlie in foil blankets to keep them warm. Charlie and Lachlan answered questions about what they'd experienced and if they had seen anyone else on the island.

The grocer, Callum, ambled up the road and coughed out a sound of relief when he saw Nessie being checked over by one of the rescuers.

"Oh, my sweet lassie." He cried happy tears into her hair as he hugged her. The man turned to Charlie, his eyes glistening. "One o' the responders said he saw her up here. I was so worried. Thank ye for keeping her safe. A dinnae ken what tae do without her."

"She's a sweet girl," Charlie said. "I'm happy she's okay."

"I'm indebted tae ye," he said with a shaky voice.

"You're absolutely not. She was such a comfort during the scariest parts of the storm. I was glad to have her by my side."

He roughly wiped the tears from his eyes with his shirt sleeve. "The missus will be so happy when she hears we've found her."

Charlie looked down to the road below. "And your store? The main road was flooded pretty badly at one point."

He nodded. "Aye. I have nae checked the store, but I suspect it will have heavy damage." He straightened and held his chin high. "But it's nothing we can't handle. We have a strong community on the island. We'll help each other and rebuild. That's just how we are."

Charlie gave him a weak smile and nodded to her house, now worse for the wear. "Count me in."

Callum held out his hand, and she took it. He squeezed tightly with reassurance. "Ye are one o' us now. We'll take care o' ye."

"Thank you."

"I best be going. The missus will be wanting tae spoil this dog rotten." He pet Nessie's head and tipped his head to say farewell.

Through the sadness, Charlie found a bright spot. Reuniting Nessie with her owner took away some of the anguish that lurked on the edges. It might have been dangerous to go out into the storm to save her, but it was worth it for this very moment.

The responders continued to run their tests to ensure Lachlan and Charlie were uninjured. As she went through it all on autopilot, she watched as more of the island people filtered up the street to check on their homes. There was a mixture of shock and sorrow for some, while others felt determined they'd do whatever it took to make the community stronger.

She was proud to be a part of that now.

"Charlie." A booming voice, heavy with a Scottish accent, rang out. Kennedy raced up the road, worry etched on his face. He took her face gently in his large, calloused hands. "I was worried sick. Gloria said she'd have me hide if anything happened tae ye."

From the corner of her eye, she could see Lachlan's reaction to their reunion. His face was filled with pain and jealousy, but he did nothing. Said nothing.

"I'm so sorry, Kennedy."

"When yer mother called tae say ye never came back, and she couldnae reach ye, I tried everything. I reached out tae everyone I ken who had a boat tae see if they would take me here, but the storm was bad at that point."

"I appreciate that. It was terrifying, but the house kept me safe."

Kennedy looked past her to the house and raised his eyebrows. He let out a low whistle. "Well then, seems like we have our work cut out for us."

Charlie cringed. "Will you be around the next couple of days to take stock of the damage? I want to know what I'm working with so I can make calls."

Kennedy nodded. "Aye. I have a few properties I need tae check on for me clients."

A no-nonsense responder holding a walkie-talkie approached them. "First boat tae the mainland leaves in thirty minutes. Will ye be boarding?"

"Yes," Lachlan said at the same time as Charlie's no. Another miserable expression crossed his face. "I have to get things sorted with the investors."

Charlie held up her hands as if she didn't have a care in the world. "Hey, you don't owe me any explanations." She tried to keep her voice in check. "You owe me nothing."

At that, Lachlan stood and took her by the elbow, tugging her to the house.

"A word?" he asked through gritted teeth.

Charlie looked over her shoulder. "I'll be a minute," she called out to Kennedy, who gave a wary wave in response.

"It's going to take a hell of a lot more than a minute," Lachlan growled before slamming the front door behind them.

CHAPTER TWENTY-FOUR

NOTHING LIKE ACTING like a Neanderthal to sway her decision.

Lachlan was spinning out of control, but he needed to give it one last shot. In thirty minutes, he'd be boarding the rescue boat back to the mainland without Charlie, leaving her to run into the arms of that brawny Scotsman who looked at her in a way that boiled his blood.

In mere moments, he would lose her. He knew she still cared, no matter how much she tried to push him away. He needed to get through to her.

Charlie shrugged his hand off her elbow. "Christ, Lachlan. What has gotten into you?"

"*You!*" He shoved a hand in his hair. "Charlie, please come home with me. We need more time."

She narrowed her eyes and crossed her arms. "And just like that, back to the demands. You want *me* to drop everything for *you*. Again!" She waved her hands around the house. "Don't you see I have something I need to take care of?"

Lachlan flinched, then shook his head. "I meant after you sort this out, so we can talk."

"There's nothing to sort out. You're on the first available ship home, and that's it. Our 'fling' is over."

A fling? *A fling?* This was anything but a fling. He could walk away from a fling, but he sure as hell couldn't walk away from her so easily.

Her sentence—full of disdain—spoke volumes. There was no changing her mind. She saw it as him going back to the life she accused him of not being able to leave, choosing to give her up instead.

She couldn't be more wrong, yet he couldn't find a way to convey that, not when he was so emotionally wrought.

"Charlie—"

"Enough, Lachlan," she said with anger, but he could hear the pain behind it.

There was still hope.

"Damn it, Charlie. I'm falling for you!" He hadn't meant for it to come out that way, but he had to break through her stubbornness to be heard.

He *needed* her to hear it before it was too late.

Charlie's arms dropped to her side, and her mouth fell open in slack surprise. She stood there, stunned speechless.

He took a tentative step forward. "I'm falling in love with you. How could I not? You've done what no one else could do for a long time: you've made me want to be a better man. Now let me show you I can be."

She shook her head as tears streamed from her eyes. A look of torture twisted her features.

He crossed the room, wanting to take her in his arms, but held back. Her guard was still up, despite her shell-shocked state. "Me asking you to come back isn't a selfish demand." He paused and reconsidered. "Well, I guess it is, but not for the reasons you think. It's not so I can get back to the business and figure us out when I have time. It's because I want to know we have a real shot. That we'd try. I don't want to wait. You made me see everything I was missing in my life, and now I can't stand going another minute without it. Without *you*."

She bit her bottom lip, looking uncertain.

"Come back with me," he pleaded. "It won't be the same without you."

"Because I'm not your assistant anymore? Or because of what grew between us?"

He stopped for a second. "Both. It won't feel right not seeing you every day, but that's not the point. The point is I want to know that I *can* see you. That I can take you to dinner. That I can hold your hand while walking in Central Park. I want you there, with me, by my side."

Charlie paused. Her mouth opened and closed, on the verge of saying something. Her face softened before her defiance came back. "Lach, I stand by what I said. You need to forget about me. Give me space." A humorless laugh escaped her. "You should probably forget me altogether. I know how you are. You haven't had time for a real relationship in the three years I've worked for you. Probably even longer."

"But I want one with you. You've made me a different man."

For a moment, she almost looked like she believed him.

She sighed. "Look, as much as I wish that were true, we both know that's easy to believe when you're disconnected from reality." Her voice went from rough to gentle. "Here, on this island with you, I was honestly convinced you and I could work. But you know as soon as we get back, our routines, responsibilities, and daily lives will make it so we revert to how things were. To prove you're a changed man, you need to face the real world and show me your feelings can survive all of that."

Determination bubbled inside his chest. If she couldn't believe him, he'd simply have to show her. "Okay."

She cocked her head. "Okay? Just like that?"

"You're wary. I get it. Your career aspirations are important to you. Of course I would understand that, and I don't want you to feel like I'm getting in the way."

"That's not all—"

"If you need some time apart to see that I can do it and that this could work, so be it. But promise me this."

She lifted her chin, trying her hardest to seem strong, but he could see her breaking right before his eyes. "What?"

Why is she doing this? Pushing me away obviously hurts her.

"When I do prove I've changed—and I will—you'll give us a fair shot."

"*If* you change, then yes."

"But not before?" He hated the desperation in his voice. He already knew her answer, but his foolish hope made him ask again.

She gave one firm shake of the head, her eyes filling with tears.

"Okay." Lachlan picked up his overnight bag and opened the front door. He turned back to her one last time. "Don't forget about me, Charlie," he pleaded quietly and closed the door behind him.

CHAPTER TWENTY-FIVE

It had been nearly six months since Charlie had heard from Lachlan. Six months since she'd watched him walk out the front door of the cottage, taking her foolish hopes with him. Six months of silence, each passing day a solid reminder that he had done exactly what she had accused him of: he went back to his life in New York and forgot about her.

Charlie had returned to New York a week after the storm, weak, weary, and heartbroken. She still had hope, but after the first month of silence, reality had settled in. She and Lachlan were done. The realization had felt like losing him all over again.

Devonny had found her curled in a ball on her bedroom floor one night, and Charlie finally told her what had actually happened on the island. After she'd finished, she had made Devonny promise never to mention his name again. Despite Devonny's tendency to promote feminism and girl power, she had simply nodded and kept her word.

Although the UX bootcamp had kept Charlie busy and gave her a bright spot in a world of dullness, she still struggled not to pick up her phone every ten seconds to see if he had called. In all those months, he never had.

Her classes and homework kept her mind off him, but in those quiet moments when she took a moment to pause and breathe, the memories of their time at the cottage came flooding back. His words, his touch, the way he made her feel.

How he told her he loved her.

It was a highlight reel constantly flashing through her mind, reminding her how he had managed to burrow his way into her heart so quickly. Charlie often wondered if she had made the right choice, or if she should have had more faith that they could make their big life changes together. There were days she was tempted to pick up the phone and call him. To hear from him.

But the fact that he never called when he said he would spoke volumes.

After months of torturing herself with thoughts of Lachlan and the notion that he had let her go so effortlessly, Charlie came to terms that she had to get on with her life. She had told him that being him with him would hold her back from what she wanted to accomplish. And somehow, even in his absence, he still was. Though, it was all her fault. She was letting her feelings for him and the disappointment that he didn't follow through paralyze her.

Hope is a bitch like that, she thought as she stepped onto the plane to Scotland. Her stomach churned at the thought of returning to the Isle of Murdina for the first time since the storm.

Am I ready for this?

After graduating from the bootcamp, Charlie had been lucky enough to land a job at one of the bootcamp's local partner tech companies. They agreed to push her start date by three weeks, so she could use the free time to revisit the cottage. There was still so much to do, and she needed every free moment she had to get it done, whether she was ready or not.

The flight attendant's voice sounded over the plane's intercom. "Ladies and gentlemen, we kindly ask you to turn off your mobile devices as we prepare for takeoff."

Charlie dug out her phone from her purse and was about to

switch it to "Airplane Mode" when a call from Devonny lit up her screen. Charlie hit the ignore button and shot Devonny a quick message saying she couldn't talk but would text when she got on the plane's Wi-Fi.

Devonny Mercado: 911

Charlie: *Just text it to me.*

Devonny was one of Charlie's more logical friends, but she sometimes had a tendency to be more dramatic than necessary.

Devonny Mercado: *Fine.*

Charlie could almost see her eye roll.

Devonny Mercado: *This is CONFIDENTIAL. It hasn't been shared with the public yet.*

Charlie watched the dots for what felt like forever. Finally, the message came through.

Devonny Mercado: *Lachlan announced he is leaving the company. Effective immediately.*

CHAPTER TWENTY-SIX

CHARLIE FELT like she had been holding her breath since Devonny's text. Lachlan had left the company weeks ago, and there still wasn't a single word from him. When she'd found out he'd resigned, she'd thought maybe he was finally going through with it, and the promise he'd made to her would actually happen.

She'd read articles about his new foundation these last few weeks and couldn't stop the swell of pride she felt for him. He did it. He'd followed through.

Yet...

Why hadn't he called? She checked her phone religiously, worried her cell service on the island was preventing him from reaching her, clutching to it like a lifeline for fear of missing his call.

As phone calls and texts from everyone else came through without a hitch, she accepted that the call from Lachlan would never come. Some damn fool she was.

Even after all that disappointment, her heart still belonged to him.

Charlie waved to the contractors leaving the cottage for the night. She only had a couple of days left on the island before she had to head back to New York, but she was thoroughly impressed with the amount they'd accomplished so far.

Another positive thing in her life despite the ache in her chest.

Charlie's cell phone rang, and her heart raced and then sank when she saw the name on the screen. "Hi, Mama."

"Hi, honey. I wanted to call and check in."

Charlie settled in at the small bistro table in the kitchen. No matter how old she was, her mother always checked in on her. "It's going great. I still have a bit to save before we can finish the cosmetic side of things, but the big-ticket items are nearly done. The contractors assured me it would be steady through the harsh winter."

"About that...I have some news."

She paused. "Everything okay?"

"Fine. Fine." Charlie could practically see her mom waving off her concerns. "I sold the house."

Charlie's stomach dropped. "What?" The house she grew up in? The house her aunt, uncle, and mom raised her in was gone?

"It was time. Living in that big ol' house alone was too much."

"But all the memories—"

"Will still live within our hearts," her mother gently reminded. "As much as I miss Violet and will miss all the wonderful memories we made in that house, there comes a time where we need to let go of our past to make way for the future. We all gotta make a little room for what's next. You know?"

"What are you saying?"

"What I'm saying is I'm giving you money from the sale to finish the cottage."

Charlie let out a breath. "But what about you? Where are you going to live?"

"I had enough money from the sale to get myself a nice little town house closer to work. There's an HOA, so no fuss in keeping it up."

"But you loved landscaping."

"I loved it because I was doing it with Aunt Violet. Now it's time for me to find my own interests. I joined a book club recently. It's been a lot of fun."

Charlie's heart softened, feeling marginally better that her mom was going on with life and building new relationships. Charlie had been so worried that once her aunt had passed, her mom would be all alone.

"Wouldn't you rather use that extra money for retirement?"

She could feel her mother's smile over the phone. "I am. I'm investing in our new vacation cottage." She paused, her voice filling with emotion. "Maybe Aunt Vi and Uncle Jon didn't get to use it as they'd hoped, but I want it to be *our* place. Somewhere we can make memories together with them in mind."

Charlie's eyes welled up with tears. "It sounds wonderful, Mama."

"Plus, you worked hard to change your career. I'm so proud of you. I know New York isn't cheap, and I don't want you sacrificing your life because the cottage became a money pit. We've sacrificed enough in our lives, haven't we?"

She smiled. "Yes. Thank you."

"Now that we got that out of the way, let's talk kitchen renovations."

Charlie laughed and spent the next half an hour chatting with her mom about how they could make the cottage their own. Each moment that passed, Charlie felt more hopeful. The future seemed brighter.

As she went to hang up the phone, her mother left her with one last parting thought. "Charlie, dear. I know this cottage meant a lot to you when you found out it was yours. I also know your time there has left a lasting memory."

Her mother had heard every heartbreaking detail when she'd returned to Georgia. Gloria had let Charlie cry it out, stroking her hair like she used to do when Charlie was a child. Through the tears, Charlie choked out how she lost her heart in a matter of days.

"I'm not sure what you're getting at."

"What I'm saying is, don't give up on love. I know I've said it to you before, and I will keep saying it until it gets into your stubborn head. Love is a special thing, and we're lucky to find it with someone whose soul matches ours in a way that changes us so completely. You did a brave thing going after your new career, putting yourself first. But..."

"But what? Spit it out."

"You went from one extreme to another. You put everyone before you, and now you're putting yourself before everyone else. You shut out everything to protect your newfound independence. Remember what I said about making a little room? Life doesn't have to be so black and white. It doesn't have to be all or nothing. You can have your cake and eat it too if you do it right."

Charlie swiped at her errant tears. "I didn't give up on love. It gave up on me."

"I wouldn't be so sure about that. Destiny has a funny way of bringing people together again. Just do one thing for me, honey. If love comes back to you, promise me you'll give it a fair shot again."

Charlie's heart clenched at the words—the same promise Lachlan had her make. "I will, Mama."

CHAPTER TWENTY-SEVEN

A SOFT BREEZE rustled Lachlan's hair as he stepped off the ferry. He inhaled the salty air and adjusted the duffel bag slung over his shoulder as he continued down the dock. His stomach was in knots. His heart raced.

He hadn't slept a wink these last six months, spending long hours at MindThrive AI to ensure it would succeed when he left. He had quietly selected a successor—someone he knew deep down would have the best interest of the company and everyone involved.

It had been nearly two weeks since he had finally walked away from MindThrive so he could put his full attention on his newest venture. Every step of the way, his fingers ached to pick up his phone and call Charlie. He wanted to tell her all about it and show he kept his word. But mostly, he wanted to hear her voice. He missed her beyond comprehension.

He felt incomplete without her.

Lachlan knew it was going to be hard when he had walked away from her. Somehow, in a matter of days, she had left a mark on him. Charlie had made him into a better man, and he wanted to show her truly he was.

A couple of days ago, he had found the nerve to call Charlie, but her phone went straight to voice mail. He wondered if maybe she'd changed her number or blocked him.

He wouldn't give up that easily. Not after everything.

She deserved more. *They* deserved more.

Lachlan just hoped he wasn't too late and that she'd kept her promise to give them a chance when he finally came back around.

Miraculously, Lachlan had managed to convince Devonny to tell him how to reach Charlie. When he found out she was on the Isle of Murdina, it all made sense why he couldn't get through to her. Devonny said she'd be back in a few days, but for Lachlan, those were a few days too many. He'd already missed her for nearly seven months. He was done waiting.

Lachlan was impressed when he stepped foot onto the main road. The town was teeming with energy. At first glance, he might not have realized it had been ravaged by a horrible storm the previous autumn.

Beyond the colorful buildings of the main street, he looked up to find the surviving trees and new flowers of the village blooming in the spring. The purple hue of heather lining the green hills in the distance danced in the breeze. It really *was* beautiful here. He was glad Charlie had fought to keep the cottage...even without his help.

Making his way through the busy main road, he skirted around tourists who stopped at the small outdoor markets full of fresh catches, artwork, and Scottish trinkets. A gorgeous red-haired dog came running up to him and rubbed her wiggling body against his legs.

"Hey, Nessie." He crouched down to give the dog a scratch. "Long time, no see. You staying out of trouble?"

Nessie licked his face in response.

He laughed. "Good girl."

She gave one last lick before running back to the grocer's. Lachlan straightened and continued his trek up the hill. Some of the waterlogged houses at the bottom were still a work in progress, but the cottages steadily got better with each one he passed.

Somehow, he could relate. In such a short time, he felt like an entirely new person, despite being a work in progress.

He pushed forward, each footstep more urgent than the last. He was eager to get to Charlie, knowing her cottage was just around the bend. His heartbeat spiked when he rounded the corner.

He stopped midstride.

There she was. Like a dream come to life.

Her thick red hair was pulled into a loose braid. She wore jean shorts, a flannel and tank, and work boots. Even in her little construction getup, she was stunning.

A few men came out of the cottage, and she handed them paperwork and gave instructions. The men nodded, grabbed tools from the back of the truck, and disappeared inside again.

Charlie took that moment of peace to close her eyes and turn her face toward the sun. Her fair skin had a bit of color on it now. Lachlan didn't think he could find her any more beautiful, but here he was, practically panting over the girl next door.

He took tentative steps toward her, not wanting to disrupt her moment. It took everything in him not to race to her and wrap her in his arms, kissing her senseless. He had practiced what he'd say a million times these last few months, but words failed him when he saw her.

"Funny to run into you here," he said quietly when he reached her.

Charlie stilled at the sound of his voice and slowly opened her eyes as if she were scared she'd wake up from a wonderful dream. She exhaled a breath, the look of shock and confusion crossing her face.

"Lachlan?" She reached up and touched his face tenderly, gauging if he was a figment of her imagination.

"I've missed you."

Her eyes misted. "I didn't think I would ever hear from you again. I was convinced, actually."

"I tried calling, but your phone went to voice mail. Devonny said you were here."

A smile lifted her lips. "So you just jumped on a transatlantic flight to talk to me?"

"Seems to be a pattern. You're worth that and more."

She dropped her hand. Her eyebrows furrowed. "Devonny said you left MindThrive weeks ago. Why didn't you call me sooner?"

He could hear the hurt in her voice, and his insides clenched knowing he was the one who did that.

"I knew you'd be a hard woman to convince that I changed, so I needed the extra time to get situated. I started the Maggio-Hart Foundation to fund an incubator. I did it, Charlie."

When he first returned to New York, he had called back his grammar school and agreed to speak to several classes. When he saw the kids' eyes brighten with amazement and interest, it clicked for him.

Lachlan had been lucky growing up in a community like that, where the school systems and the parents were encouraging. But not every kid was as fortunate as him or the kids he had spoken to.

Matteo, for example.

Somehow, Matteo had beaten the odds of his upbringing and made something of himself. Sometimes it was hard to fathom Matteo's former life and how he found it within himself to make it to college and succeed in technology.

But he had done it, and he had thrived.

Maybe more bright minds could be fostered if someone just gave them a chance. Lachlan wanted to be the one to give it to them.

"I put everything I had into it," he continued. "Took out my stock and bonds. Poured those funds into it. I took a big swing. Within a few months, the foundation sprang up a handful of incubators in locations throughout New York City. We even created after-school programs for kids in grammar school and high school to expose them to the world of technology. And because many of these kids have hard lives, we set up transportation so they never have to miss out."

"Wow. Lachlan. That's amazing. I read a little about it, but I didn't realize how much you've accomplished already."

He beamed at her praise. "We're really making a difference in these kids' lives."

Charlie took stock of him, eyeing his jeans, T-shirt, and casual button-down with the sleeves rolled to his forearms. "No more suits and ties for you?"

He shook his head. "I'm a new man all around." He reached out and pulled her in for a hug, taking a deep breath of her flowery-peppery scent. "I told you I would change. And at the end of the day, my feelings for you remained." Lachlan pushed a stray strand of hair from her face. "I'm in love with you, Charlie. Always will be."

She tightened her grip around him, and her breath escaped her in a harsh whoosh.

Lachlan looked into those stunning green eyes he could only dream about these last seven months. "It's been hell not having you with me through all these big decisions, but I knew you needed the space to grow too. I'm here now, a changed man, because of you. You helped me see I could be more. That I could change my life if I wanted to. It's been a long time since I felt this way. Free. Exhilarated. Hungry for life."

Charlie searched his face. "I can see it in your eyes. You look happy."

"Can you also see how much I want to be with you, Charlie?" When she paused, Lachlan's blood ran cold. "Tell me it isn't too late. That *I'm* not too late."

A slow smile reached her full lips. She pulled him in and crushed her mouth against his, giving him a passionate kiss like her life depended on it. He felt the emotion behind it, the months of pent-up longing coming alive with each swipe of her tongue. She broke the kiss, and he rested his forehead against hers.

"When I didn't hear from you, I thought you had moved on," she admitted.

"Never. You were in my thoughts every second. Every day."

Her eyes misted with happy tears. "Good. Because I'm in love with you too, Lach." She looked at him as if he were her whole world.

His heart swelled with hope. "Will you keep your promise to me? To give this a fair shot?"

"Absolutely."

Relief washed over him as he took her hand and squeezed it. "Let's see what you've done with the place."

He led her to the cottage, the place where the two of them truly began. The place where he had opened up to her and discovered more about himself and the possibilities he could have for his life.

Charlie's aunt had been right. The cottage really was magical. It gave him two of the most important things he could have ever hoped for: discovering purpose in his work again and finding the woman he loved. He had jumped on a plane and endured a terrible storm to find it, and he wouldn't have had it any other way.

"Maybe we can start by getting me caught up on everything I've missed," he suggested. "I want to hear it all. Every detail about the house, the bootcamp, your new career. Everything."

She beamed again. "I'd like that."

And all felt right in his world.

***

Thank you for reading! Did you enjoy?

Please Add Your Review! You can sign up for the City Owl Press newsletter to receive notice of all book releases!

And don't miss more romance like INTERNSHIP WITH THE DEVIL by City Owl Author, Jaqueline Snowe. Turn the page for a sneak peek!

SNEAK PEEK OF INTERNSHIP WITH THE DEVIL

BY JAQUELINE SNOWE

"Hi, I'm supposed to meet Mr. Anderson in about ten minutes. Could you point me in the right direction?" I held my arms against my stomach, hoping it looked natural and not like my nerves were shot to hell. This internship was a dream come true.

"You're going to want to head down this hallway, turn right once you pass the locker room." The security guard's smile stretched across his weathered face. His nametag read *Barry*.

I liked Barry instantly. I waved, thanking him as I headed to meet my temporary boss.

I checked my watch—I still had time. I probably looked like a damn lunatic, walking and smiling at everything. Despite being awful at playing sports, I loved them. I was clumsy, and got way too winded when I walked upstairs, but watching football and baseball for hours? I'd do that for days. And now I was going to be able to work with athletes. Learning from athletic trainers at the college level. Hell. Yes.

I turned right after the locker room. The offices had names on them and I looked until I found Brock Anderson. I reviewed what I learned about him before I knocked. He played college football, but only three years in the NFL, before suffering a career ending injury.

He was fairly young, just twenty-eight, an alumnus of the school, and was known to whip athletes into amazing shape. He got his masters in Athletic Training. I was going to learn so damn much.

With a smile that I had been told was too big for my face, I knocked on the door. I waited, hearing voices from within the office and froze when the door opened.

No. This couldn't be.

It was The Asshole.

From the bar a week ago.

No.

My stomach about fell through my ass, like gravity had given up on me at that moment. He stared at me, those scary blue eyes seeing through me. Maybe he worked here. No way this was Mr. Anderson. The pictures showed a clean shaven, handsome guy who maybe didn't smile. This guy had shaggy hair, dark beard, no smile at all. My gaze darted to his polo, which stretched tight across his chest. And what a chest it was.

Focus, Grace.

Shit.

Anderson was embroidered underneath the school's logo.

Shit. Damn. Balls.

He was my new supervisor.

My fist clenched.

"Uh, hi. I'm Grace Turner." I held out my sweaty hand, hoping the trembling wasn't too obvious. I needed to get off to a good start. My career goals were important. More important than this guy being a dick. So, I waited. And waited. And waited.

His lips turned downward. So much so that it had to hurt his face. My hand still hung between us, awkward and a mixture of embarrassment to the tenth degree. He moved one of his hands to scratch his jaw, bringing my attention to his incredible jawline.

I dropped my hand. I couldn't handle the flip-flopping going on in my stomach, and when I got uncomfortable, word vomit ensued. Hence, why I decided to attempt being friendly. "Are you Brock

Anderson? I'm the one who received the internship for the season. I'm Grace. I'm so excited for this opportunity."

I'd introduced myself. Again. And, he still hadn't said a word. Someone moved into view from his office and gave me a small wave. I returned the gesture to the older gentleman and that was when Asshole Anderson spoke.

"Excuse me." He motioned with his large wrist for me to leave the office.

I stepped back, shocked, and gasped when he shut the door in my face. What. The. Hell. I pinched my nose, taking deep breaths. I counted to three a couple of times and calmed myself down, but then loud, angry voices carried through the door. It was him, his voice brasher and deeper than anyone else's. So, I did what anyone would do. I listened.

"I refuse to train immature people. Look, Victor—" Someone interrupted him, Victor, my guess. I couldn't decipher what Victor said, but Brock Asshole Anderson didn't like it. Not one bit.

"She was the best option? I doubt it. Come on. Assign her to someone else. I don't have time for an attention-hungry little girl. I want someone serious who works their ass off. Not her." His voice carried through the door, stabbing me like a bunch of knives.

Attention-hungry.

Little girl.

Not serious.

Not her.

Hell. No. My fists clenched at my sides, my heart raced way past the point of comfort, and I contemplated a million ways to kill him. But, that wouldn't help my goals, and I was that tenacious, annoying person who, when told they couldn't do something, determined to prove them wrong.

He'd judged me. Entirely incorrectly, but a judgment all the same. Maybe he remembered me from the bar. Sure, I tried flirting after a dare from my best friend, and he made it clear he wasn't interested. Quite clear. If he remembered me from that night, it didn't bode well for me. It wasn't like I threw myself at him. I just offered to buy him a drink and after a quick look up and down, he laughed and said absolutely not. Shame and regret clogged my throat.

Without waiting to hear what else was said, I took life by the balls. I had learned from a young age that I had to fight for what I wanted in life. Happiness? That was a choice I had to work at every day. I sensed my mom cheering for me from above when I pounded on the door, hard.

The voices stopped, someone letting out a curse. Then, the door opened. Brad grimaced at my expression. I had been told I had a fire in my eyes when I got pissed. I had more than fire right now. I was a raging inferno. "As much as I enjoyed your polite, pleasant conversation, I earned the internship."

Brock Asshole Anderson stared me down.

If he wanted to see me squirm, that was too damn bad. I crossed my arms and raised my eyebrows in challenge.

Victor, clearly not the alpha in this situation, gave me a quick nod and strolled out. "We'll talk later, Brock."

That left me and him. He blinked at me, assessing me, sighing so deeply it took a minute for it to leave his lungs. He had to have massive lungs, right? He was massive. The sarcastic side of my brain then chipped in, he also was a massive asshole.

"Don't wear that here." He scolded my carefully planned outfit—a professional black dress—and my skin tingled with embarrassment. "Wear team gear."

He continued, "Be here every day at seven. You'll have a quick lunch and the time changes every day. You'll leave at four." He moved from the doorway to sit at his desk, shuffling through papers.

I cringed. My classes began at four Tuesdays and Thursdays, but I was not going to give him any excuse. I hoped my professors accepted me being tardy or I would be screwed.

"Okay."

"Once games start, you're expected at every home and away game. I'll have my secretary print you a schedule. If you're late once, you're done." He looked up, eyes smoldering. "Absolutely none of the flirting shit or dating any of the players. Is that clear?"

"Yes," I croaked, still shocked at his crassness. His words erased any doubt over whether he remembered that night. But I wouldn't acknowledge it. I remained at the doorframe, awkward, uncomfortable, angry, and sweaty. I chewed on my bottom lip, unsure what to do. His jaw clenched, his gaze briefly going to my mouth. It was so quick I almost missed it.

He cleared his throat, darting his gaze to the chair in front of him. "Sit."

I obeyed like a desperate, foolishly hopeful girl. I needed, wanted, *dreamed* of this chance. He would not ruin it. It was only four months. I could put up with the Asshole for four months. "We'll do a tour of the stadium today after we set some ground rules."

I nodded but twisted my hands in my lap.

He stood, grabbed a radio and a clipboard, then marched out the door so quickly I barely had time to keep up. "Ain't my fault you wore those shoes. I don't slow down for anyone. If you can't keep up, I'll consider you lazy."

And that was how I spent my morning.

I walked faster than I ever had, my shoes clicking on the cement floor. He showed me the offices where the trainers, EMTs, and coaches spent most of their time. I visited the various gyms and weight rooms, the mats, the pool, and the film room. We walked around the track at least twenty times, going over where the water house was, the spickets, the hoses, and the water bottles. It was noon when we finished the tour and blisters upon blisters formed on my ankles. But, I would not let him win. Not today.

"The Special Teams group is out practicing. They need water. Consider this your first assignment." He narrowed his eyes and had an innocent expression cross his face as I eyed the distance between the field and water house, then my footwear choice. It specifically said on the email from my counselor that I would only meet to *talk* today. There wasn't supposed to be any duties until classes began. Joke was on me. This was an internship with the devil.

"Okay," I said, finding a deep determination inside myself. I had filled countless coolers in high school. I worked football games, volleyball tournaments, and baseball games. I had taped ankles, cleaned wounds, held hands, and watched athletes cry. I could do this.

He whistled at someone and strode off in the other direction.

This was a test. And I would pass it.

I made my way to the storage room back inside the stands. I pulled out all three and carried them to the water house. It was open, thank god, because I refused to ask for help. I began filling the first one.

With it filled, I added ice. It was a blistering summer afternoon, and the players had to be dying. Hell, I was sweating my ass off, but my dress was so dark sweat wouldn't be noticeable. The cooler was heavier than most trays I carried waitressing. I lugged it to the bench, sweat dripping down my face. One down, two to go.

I did it again, and on the third one, my arms burned. Shit. This job required me to have more muscles, and more muscles meant gym time. Ugh. I was wiping my neck with the back of my hand when someone snuck behind me.

"Excuse me, but I'm not used to seeing people dressed like this on the field." I twisted to see a friendly, grinning man. He stood at least six feet, dressed in khaki shorts and a navy polo. What was it with football people and polos? They were not stylish, at all.

"Ah, yes. About that. I was under the impression I would get a tour and that's it. But I officially began my internship today. I'm Grace Turner." I held out my hand, and he took it in his large one.

"Hi, Grace Turner. I'm Logan Rice. Nice to meet the new intern. Congrats. I've heard it's hard as hell to get picked for it." His voice was gentle and reassuring.

I couldn't help but smile at him.

"Thank you. I hate to brag but I worked hard to get it. Spent last year shadowing the volleyball AT and did clinical hours at the rehab center. Hence, why I'm in this dress hauling water coolers onto the field. You're the defense coordinator, right? Started two years ago and could be credited for having one of the best defenses in the Midwest?"

"I like a woman who knows her stuff." He winked. Aw hell. It was such an old-fashioned thing, but damn. "But yes, that's me."

"You're so young, though." Hello, word vomit. "When I picture defense coordinators, I picture a bunch of old guys with beer bellies. You surprised me. That's all. Good for you." I hope that saved me from more embarrassment. I'd had enough for the day, thank you very much. But, karma enjoyed messing with me.

He grinned, a twinkle in his eye. "You aren't entirely wrong. I am young, but, to quote you, I worked my ass off to get here."

"Good for you," I said again, awkwardly repeating myself. We shared a smile. I glanced at the players on the field working on kicks and plays. The combination of the sounds, smells, teamwork from every staff member flowed so smoothly. The sense of belonging helped fuel the void not having a family left. This already felt like home. "How long have you been working with the team?"

"Oh, a couple years. I played in college and didn't want to go through the draft. Loved the sport and knew the coach. Voila." He held out his hands in a gesture I used often.

I laughed, my shoulders finally relaxing. "Well, I'm glad to find a friendly face here. I'm going to have my work cut out for me." I sighed, looking around the field and found Asshole Anderson glaring, and I mean, *glaring* at me. His piercing stare hit me, hard. I forced myself not to flinch.

Logan followed my gaze and let out a slow whistle. "So you're paired up with Anderson? How's that going?"

"Yup." I popped the 'p' at the end of the word.

He grimaced for a second. Then he ran a hand through his hair, scrunching up his face. "Damn." He shook his head, this time smiling. "He's one of the best, but he's a real dick."

I burst out laughing. "I'm not sure if this is a test or not. If I agree with you, you might tell him and I'd be fired. If I defend him, I look like a brownnoser. So, I'll choose this moment to make my exit. Nice meeting you, Logan."

"You too, Grace Turner." He winked at me again.

I bid farewell and found Asshole Anderson walking my way. I tried to hide my wince. I refused to show him weakness. But damn. I needed ice. I began to ask him what else he wanted me to do, but he interrupted me. Rudely, crassly, and I wanted to punch him.

His jaw tensed as his hooded eyes narrowed into slits. His rough voice hardly more than a growl. "You can go now."

That was all he said. No good job, or nice work. No critiques or directions for the next time to show up. He spun and walked away without a backward glance.

Screw that.

I strode after him, ignoring the awful sour feeling in my gut.

"Mr. Anderson?" I yelled.

He halted.

I walked over to him, fists clenched. Should I call him Mr. Anderson? Brock? I had no freaking clue. "I did everything you asked without complaint. When do I show up next?"

He whipped around, his teeth clenched for reasons beyond me. "Tomorrow."

"Seven?" Excitement and dread poured through me. I would get great experience starting early, but I knew without a doubt, this was going to be hell.

He nodded, looking at me with disdain. "Wear more appropriate clothing tomorrow and don't be late."

I nodded, not willing to feel guilty about my outfit. He was a mean, unhappy man. Screw him—I was here for football and a potential career.

I checked my Fitbit app on my phone as I limped to my car. I walked over seven miles that morning. I groaned into my fist as I hobbled out the main gate.

Gilly called and I immediately called her back, telling her

everything. She gasped, moaned, and cursed at all the right parts. She demanded we go pick out new clothing. Of course, I gave in. I had no choice. The extra money I made waitressing was going to go toward a new wardrobe, and although the job was a dream, I wasn't wild about my new uniform. There was no cool way to wear polos.

Gilly assured me a push-up bra and tight pants would help, but I shooed her. I chose athletic yoga pants, reasonable khaki shorts, and five school football tees, polos, and tank tops. I was set clothing wise. Emotionally? I was a few tacos and margaritas short of a fiesta.

"I can't wait to see you kick ass," Gilly said over wine later that night. "You earned this chance and you'll prove him wrong. I know it."

Her brother, our third roommate, sipped his beer, and nodded along with his sister. They were my chosen family and their support meant so much.

My email pinged with my new insane schedule. The internship was paid, but, due to Asshole Anderson starting me two weeks early, I had double shifts six days a week. I would work nine hours with him, and seven hours at the steakhouse. Goodbye social life. Goodbye world. It might be near impossible, but the challenge lit me up inside.

He wanted to be a dick?

Game on, Anderson.

* * *

Don't stop now. Keep reading with your copy of INTERNSHIP WITH THE DEVIL by City Owl Author, Jaqueline Snowe.

And find more from Sofia Sawyer at
www.sofiasawyer.com

Want even more romance? Try INTERNSHIP WITH THE DEVIL by City Owl Author, Jaqueline Snowe, and find more from Sofia Sawyer at www.sofiasawyer.com

* * *

Grace Turner scores the opportunity of a lifetime interning with an Ex-NFL player. But working under Brock Anderson turns out to be the job from hell.

The hometown hero turned athletic trainer has a reputation as the best in his field, but his volatile personality makes working with him miserable.

Despite the animosity between them, he's highly respected in his field and interning under him could mean everything for her career.

The *long* days, *longer* nights, injuries, and busses filled with smelly athletes are the easy part.

The biggest battle is the unwarranted attraction to Brock that she can't seem to shake.

But as Grace spends more and more time with her brooding boss, she uncovers that his abrasive nature is deep rooted in his grief—something she's no stranger to.

The glimpses of the man beneath the harsh exterior Brock presents to the world leave Grace conflicted in her feelings for him. As the internship draws to a close, Grace is faced with a choice that could set her future on an entirely new course.

* * *

Please sign up for the City Owl Press newsletter for chances to win special subscriber-only contests and giveaways as well as receiving information on upcoming releases and special excerpts.

All reviews are **welcome** and **appreciated**. Please consider leaving one on your favorite social media and book buying sites.

Escape Your World. Get Lost in Ours! Romance and speculative fiction from City Owl Press at www.cityowlpress.com.

ACKNOWLEDGMENTS

When I passed my driver's test at the ripe age of seventeen, my father said to me, "Travel as often as you can before life's responsibilities get in the way." I took that advice to heart, and in my teenage years and early twenties, I did just that.

Scraping by on minimum wage jobs or having nearly no time to take off due to working full time while going to college, I often settled for quick road trips or mini trips with my friends. We always found a way to make every moment an adventure, no matter how seemingly insignificant.

Fast forward sixteen years later, and I've been fortunate to live a life that lets me travel far and wide. More importantly, I was lucky enough to marry a man who also loves to explore. In the ten years we've been together, we've traveled to roughly 18 states and 10 countries so far.

Travel is a huge part of my life, and I want to hold on to those experiences, memories, and hopes as tightly as I can. What better way to do that than to let those memories live on forever in my stories? Thus, I made a choice to write travel-inspired books such as *One Stormy Night*.

Although the island and town are fictional, I crafted the setting from my own memories traveling to Edinburgh and the highlands (plus my dream to visit the Isle of Skye one day). I hope I captured that exciting feeling of being somewhere completely new and how it can change your perspective about your place in the world. I also hope it transports you to some place far away in moments when you can't physically travel.

I want to thank my parents for always encouraging me to see the world, and my friends, Ashley Porges and Tonianne Lisanti, for being my first consistent travel buddies way back when. Also, thank you to my husband, Jim Sweeney, for having patience when I neurotically over plan our trips (down to the minute), take an obnoxious number of pictures, and spend each night writing down all the experiences from the day so I never forget.

And, of course, I want to show my appreciation for all the people who helped this book come to be. Thank you to Jana Hanson from Metamorphosis Literary Agency for believing in me and Mary Cain and Tina Moss from City Owl Press for helping me through the editing and publishing process.

To my readers: I hope you enjoy this adventure as much as I did writing it!

ABOUT THE AUTHOR

When Sofia Sawyer's fifth-grade teacher handed her a journal, encouraging her to keep writing, she vowed she always would. A lifelong storyteller, Sofia writes contemporary romances featuring tenacious women who won't stop until they get their happily ever after.

Based in Charleston, S.C., she follows her wanderlust whenever she can to new and exciting places, often finding story ideas throughout her travels.

When she isn't reading, writing, or jet-setting across the globe, you can find Sofia playing with her dog, taking advantage of the amazing Charleston restaurant scene, hiking, or hanging at the beach.

Sofia is represented by Jana Hanson from Metamorphosis Literary Agency.

Sign up for her newsletter at www.sofiasawyer.com/newsletter

 facebook.com/sofiasawyerwriter

twitter.com/sofia_sawyer

instagram.com/sofiasawyerwriter

pinterest.com/sofiasawyerwriter

ABOUT THE PUBLISHER

City Owl Press is a cutting edge indie publishing company, bringing the world of romance and speculative fiction to discerning readers.

Escape Your World. Get Lost in Ours!

www.cityowlpress.com